THE PREACHER'S SON

THE
PREACHER'S SON

Elizabeth Gill

severn
House

This first world edition published in Great Britain 2005 by
SEVERN HOUSE PUBLISHERS LTD of
9–15 High Street, Sutton, Surrey SM1 1DF.
This first world edition published in the USA 2005 by
SEVERN HOUSE PUBLISHERS INC of
595 Madison Avenue, New York, N.Y. 10022.

British Library Cataloguing in Publication Data

Gill, Elizabeth, 1950-
    The preacher's son
    1.   Methodist Church (Great Britain) - Clergy - Fiction
    2.   County Durham (England) - Social life and customs -
         19th century - Fiction
    I.   Title
    823.9'14 [F]

    ISBN 0-7278-6235-9

Except where actual historical events and characters are being
described for the storyline of this novel, all situations in this
publication are fictitious and any resemblance to living persons
is purely coincidental.

Typeset by Palimpsest Book Production Limited,
Polmont, Stirlingshire, Scotland.
Printed and bound in Great Britain by
MPG Books Ltd., Bodmin, Cornwall.

One

It seemed fitting to Josh that he and Emma should meet for the last time beside the thorn tree under which John Wesley had preached so long ago. It was peaceful there, just outside the village where his father, Christopher Castle, was the Methodist minister.

Beyond it was a bridge above a clear tumbling river which was studded with round grey stones, and the fields went up on either side, green now that it was early summer, and the neat walls dividing them were all that stayed the sheep from wandering.

How could anybody leave the dale in summer, he wondered? Dog roses spotted the hedgerows with pink, cow parsley and elderflower were creamy lace, the may and blackthorn were thick white and pink, the blue sky was cloudless, and for days and days the sun had shone down relentlessly.

It was early evening, the shadows were long, the sky was clear, and Josh wanted to linger. Emma didn't say anything to him. He wanted her to tell him how much she cared for him. He wanted to make undying declarations of love to her, but he should not. He was going away for two years and it was too long to ask anything of anyone, and it was not as if he would be able to afford to come home during that time.

He wanted more than anything in the world to ask her to wait for him, but it seemed so dishonourable, to hold somebody to you because you were going away to do what you wanted to do, and she had to stay there and put up with her drunken father and her stupid mother. He felt guilty even

1

thinking of her parents like that. He wished he and Emma could run away, not to Bristol, somewhere much further, but he could not.

It wasn't that he felt God was calling him, it was nothing dramatic like that, it was just that he didn't know how to not go, how to stay here and not become a minister. His parents had urged him to go, told him how proud they were of him, and the people of the circuit had raised money so that he could become ordained.

He could not help this overwhelming need to try to do something useful, something to enable people to lead better lives. Now, that did sound pompous, and it was not what he meant. He wanted to help, he wanted to aid the difficult lives they led, not to change them but to support them in what they would do.

Nobody spoke. The time was going past very quickly. It was his last evening at home. In a way he wished it had rained, it might be easier to go, and then he thought of how green the steep hills looked in the rain, how it washed the walls of the fields to shining, and he knew that it wouldn't make any difference. How could you leave in snow, when the whole area was a study in grey and white, or in autumn, when the brown, gold and lime-coloured leaves floated down the river, dusk came early and sent you off home to the sitting-room fire as the sun went down splendidly between the trees and the willow herb turned to tall wisps of fluff in the hedgerows? Down by the stream, small brown birds flew low over the water and the rosehips glowed like bright-red beads among the greenery.

They walked into the middle of the bridge and Emma leaned over and gazed down into the water and the sunlight turned her red hair to flames. She had blue eyes and creamy skin and he felt very sorry for all those men whom Emma Meikle didn't love, because she was so astonishingly beautiful.

This was not why he loved her, he told himself, he loved her because there was nothing except her, nothing but the fact that he was leaving. Sometimes he resented it very much.

'You will write to me?' he said.

She nodded but didn't reply, and when she turned to him, her eyes were full of tears. Josh couldn't help himself then.

'I love you so very much. I will love you until I die.'

He kissed her. He knew very well that he shouldn't have, had promised himself that he wouldn't, but he wasn't sorry that he had. She put her arms around his neck and returned the pressure of his lips, and it was the sweetest thing in the whole world.

'Wait for me.'

'I will.'

'When I come back, if you would like, we could be married.'

Her blue eyes gleamed.

'That's everything I want,' she said.

It did not occur to Emma until she was walking home, blind with tears, that you shouldn't say such things and that even if Josh had God's ear, which she wasn't convinced he had, to put all your eggs in one basket like that was a terrible mistake, misjudgement, a tempting of fate, which she would never do, but at the time all that had been important was to let him know how much she cared.

She knew also that, if he were to become a minister, he must go, and she knew he wanted that, but she needed him to stay, more than anything in the world.

Home was the Grey Bull, one of half a dozen pubs which sat around the square in the village. Her father ran the pub and he was the kind of jolly, hard-drinking man the local farmers, labourers and quarrymen seemed to like. He was always there, merry, joking, talking, full of beer. They came because of his conversation and because the beer was well kept and possibly some of the young men came hoping to catch a glimpse of one of his four daughters. They never did. Her mother did not like them to go into the front of the house.

It was the middle of the evening. The pub was full. Emma went up the back street and in by the yard. It was quite a big house by local standards, stone built, on the end of the row. It had four bedrooms, four rooms downstairs, two of which were given over to the pub, which left only the kitchen and one other room, and since their mother was horrified by the idea of dining in the kitchen, the other room was the combined dining/sitting room, and with six of them, the dining table and chairs and a settee and two easy chairs in it, the room seemed a lot smaller than it was.

Not that they had much time to sit about. They had no help, her father would not pay for it, he said there were sufficient of them to manage everything. She and Lucy, the sister nearest to her in age, and her mother, did everything but run the public side, and late at night, when her father had taken himself to bed, they would clear up.

Sometimes it took two hours, and it was late and dark and cold by then, the nights were so clear. Even Rosamund would help, though Emma wished she wouldn't, she was fifteen and inclined to sulk.

Emma could see how tired their mother became, and very often when they went to bed, she and Lucy would lie in the narrow bed which was theirs and they would hear raised voices from their parents' bedroom next door, and then her mother crying and her father shouting and sometimes other noises which made her pull a pillow over her head to shut everything out. She and Lucy very often huddled together until the shouting died down and there in the silence they would try to go to sleep.

It was very late indeed when they finished their work that night but it was only when they went upstairs that Lucy had the opportunity to ask, 'Did you see Josh?'

And then she told her. There was a brief silence, after which Lucy said into the faint light of their one candle, 'I thought he was going to ask you to marry him.'

'On what? He can't take me with him.'

'But he's going away for such a long time,' Lucy said.

Emma lay awake in the darkness, remembering those words, wishing she could run after Josh, beg him not to go or to take her with him.

They had known one another for two years, since his father had been the minister there. Before that she had not imagined there were boys like him. She had thought they were all foul-

4

mouthed workmen who threw lascivious looks across the street at her, shouted obscenities when they were drunk and did not dare to look when they were sober.

She had not seen men in control of themselves before. Her father was led by his desires, the quarrymen and labourers by poverty and the need to do gruelling work just to survive. When she met Josh – and it was a most unlikely meeting at the house of one of her mother's friends, Mrs Richmond, who was a Methodist and had been ill – she was amazed. In the main, the Catholics, the Anglicans and the Methodists led separate lives, and her knowledge of Methodist ministers was to see Josh's father in the distance, a spare, black-clad figure. She knew that they did not drink, did not dance, did not have any fun, that they were narrow-minded, penny-pinching and pious, so she could not believe that the young man before her in Mrs Richmond's sitting room was one of them.

He was seventeen. Most lads of seventeen that she knew were ignorant, stupid, proud of how little they knew. He was there with his father. He was standing with a cup and saucer in his hand and he looked at her in a generally open, friendly and enquiring way and asked whether she read much. Luckily there were several people in the room, so she was able to talk to him. A boy who read books. He was bound to be dull. And a minister's son. There was obviously no help for him. Only, he wasn't dull. He was also tall, fair, slender, spoke in a polite accent and had the audacity to say to her softly when she was about to leave, 'May I see you again?'

She tried to laugh it off.

'My father is the landlord of the Grey Bull. I doubt our paths will meet at all.'

'So that's who you are,' he said. 'My father says you're the bonniest girl in the dale.'

Emma looked with new respect at the minister, who was talking at the other side of the room and now, as though he had heard, looked across. She thought a shadow passed over his face, but it could have been nothing more than the way that the day was changing from sunshine to rain beyond the windows.

She should have said no, right from the beginning, but she did not know how. They did not see one another often, and though neither of them said as much, they both knew that it had to be a secret. Their families would not have liked it. Lucy was the only person she confided in.

She wished to be different for him, to be respectable, to be anybody other than the daughter of a publican, a gambler, a drunk. Her father would bet on anything, horses, dogs, which way a tossed coin would fall, and he lost all the time, so there was never any money.

Joshua Castle was the one light in her life and it made her think better of herself, because, although she knew she was beautiful, she did not think it was for her beauty alone that he admired her. She could make him laugh. She thought he liked being with her and it was not that he was there for what it could get him. They didn't touch.

She knew also that his life was not easy. Whether he had decided for himself that he would become a minister or whether it had always been expected of him, she did not know, only that his life was guided by things she knew nothing of, prayers, discipline, restraint. She came, in time, to be glad and sorry for that restraint, because the day arrived when they walked alone by the river and she slipped and he caught her and they were close and he didn't let go of her. Looking into his eyes, Emma thought she saw the fight that she had seen dozens of men lose before it started. He did nothing.

She said, 'Aren't you ever going to try and kiss me?' and he looked apologetic and released her and didn't look at her for a few moments, and she watched the sweep of his lashes before he looked back at her and said, 'If I did, I should never want to stop, and then where would we be?'

'I don't understand.'

That was when he told her that he was going to Bristol to be ordained so that he could become a minister like his father. That was the day all Emma's hopes ceased. He would never be allowed to marry her. They were too far apart in every possible respect. God did not let such things happen.

*   *   *

When Josh got back, everybody had gone to bed. He walked slowly up the steep flight and into the tiny back bedroom which he had to himself, and listened to the silence.

The curtains were open and through the window he could see the sheep in the fields beyond becoming darker shapes as the sun set behind the hills and the night sky settled in behind them. He heard the door and turned in surprise. It was his brother, Wesley.

There were only eighteen months between them. Wesley had grown such a lot lately that he was nearly as tall as Josh. He stood awkwardly in the doorway.

'I wish you weren't going,' he said.

Wes wasn't given to saying things like that, and they were both silenced by it.

'So do I,' Josh said, grateful for the confidence.

Wesley came in, closing the door.

'I thought you wanted to. Did you change your mind?'

Josh sighed.

'No, I never really wanted to,' he said.

'Why didn't you say, then?'

Josh left the window.

'I didn't like to disappoint Father or Mother. I have to go.'

'But you do want to be a minister?'

Josh sat down on the bed.

'I'm not sure,' he said. 'It's always been assumed that I would be, since Father and Grandfather were.'

'Is that necessarily a recommendation?'

'It just never occurred to me that I could do something else.'

'It occurs to me.'

'Does it?' Josh looked at him with fresh interest. He would miss Wes, he hadn't known until now. 'What would you do?'

'I don't know. Anything that's different.' Wesley looked anxiously at him and it was a moment that Josh would not forget. 'You will write to me, won't you?'

'Wes, you never write to anybody.'

'You never left home before,' his brother pointed out.

Two

It had not occurred to Josh that Bristol would be so different. He knew very well that Bristol was a big city, a port,
prosperous in parts, poor in other parts, just like any big place;
it was his introduction to it that astonished him. He had never
deluded himself that he came from anything other than a very
modest background, whether his parents had chosen it because
of their religion, he was not quite sure. Poverty was part of
a minister's calling, and he expected to lodge with people of
similar social standing, but when he arrived in the very fashionable terrace of large Georgian houses, he was surprised
and uncomfortable.

Diarmud Matthews had sent the carriage to the railway
station for him. The house was lavishly furnished and vast.
There were uniformed servants. Mr and Mrs Matthews wore
expensive clothes.

Josh was too astounded other than to utter his thanks to the
well-dressed couple before him, but when the door opened
behind him he turned and stared.

'Patience, come in,' her father said. 'Come and meet Joshua
Castle.'

She was nothing like Josh had ever seen before. She wore
a gown so simple that it must have cost a pitman's wages for
several months, and pearls, a double row, going from small
to slighter larger around her long and creamy neck. She had
golden hair smoothed back away from her face, and bright
blue eyes, and she came forward confidently, as Josh had
never seen a girl do, and put out her hand, and she said in a
flawless accent, 'Mr Castle. How very nice to meet you.'

Never before had Josh been ashamed of his clothes, his

8

accent, his poverty. He had always been proud of the way that his parents had chosen to live. Now he was out of place. He took the proffered hand and tried to smile and speak normally, but it was impossible. The women in Weardale were farmers' wives and daughters, or those of workmen. They were, for the most part, socially on his level or below. He had never met the daughter of a rich man. He had no idea what to say to her.

Later he was ushered upstairs. He had a huge bedroom to himself with a four-poster bed, wardrobes, thick rugs, a wall-paper covered in birds, which he really liked, and his bedroom had doors which opened out on to a balcony from which he could see right around the crescent.

It was far from his experience and not at all what he had come to Bristol for. As he stood outside, feeling a very long way from home, there was a polite knock on the door and Patience put her head round it and said, 'May I come in?'

He moved back into the room.

'It's a lovely view,' he said, not knowing what else to say.

'I have the feeling you think we are very frivolous,' she said.

This was rather too near to be comforting.

'Not at all.'

'My father gives the wrong impression, I think. He is embarrassed because his family has always been wealthy. They can't help it,' she said, with a ready smile. 'They are just good at making money, but he does put it to use. He's built schools and churches, helped a lot of people, he just doesn't tell anybody. We are so pleased to have you here, to be able to offer you somewhere to stay while you study. My mother is very pleased with you, you're just what she had in mind.'

That made him laugh, and reminded him again of Emma.

'Mother wanted a son so he could be a minister.'

'You could do a great deal.'

'I haven't the conscience for it somehow. Shall I send some-one to help with your unpacking?'

Josh, thinking of his few shabby clothes, declined this, and she went off saying, 'Dinner is in an hour. Will you be able to find your way to the dining room?'

He assured her he would, but was rather taken aback when

9

some time later, having put on the least worn of his suits, he descended and found that a dozen fashionably dressed people had been invited to dinner, and the dining room was resplendent with chandeliers, crystal glasses, silver running the whole length of the table, and the food was so good that he could not help enjoying himself.

Their friends were interesting people. The talk did not stop. He liked it so much he could not help thinking of home, small cold rooms, getting up very early, going to bed the same, food that tasted all alike. He longed for Emma and the village and his family, in particular for Wes, and when he had excused himself, saying that he was tired after his journey, he sat down at the pretty writing desk before the window, with lamps which cast more light than he was used to, and he wrote to Wes and then to Emma, saving her for last, before he went to sleep, and it gave him such comfort to describe his journey and what he had found there. He felt close to her, as though he were addressing her almost in person.

His bed was the most comfortable he had ever known. He fell into a sweet deep sleep.

When Josh had gone to bed and the guests had left for home, Patience lingered downstairs, walking around the conservatory until her mother found her there.

'So,' her mother said, 'what do you think of Mr Castle?'

Patience giggled.

'I don't understand what he's talking about and I had the awful feeling that he would ask us whether we use a lot of coal on our fires. And his clothes.'

Her mother shuddered.

'We must do something about that. I think your father could tactfully get him into something which shows off his good looks to advantage. He's a very intelligent young man. With help he could go far, do a great deal. You could take him out tomorrow, let him see Bristol.'

'He'll never want to go back to the north again,' Patience said.

*   *   *

Emma missed Josh so much that she didn't really notice things were getting worse until the night when her father told them they were moving. Her mother had not been told in advance, she could see, she looked startled.

'Pack your things,' he said. 'I've hired a cart to come late tomorrow night.'

That meant they were going without paying any of the debts or the bills which had flooded in and were even now wedged behind the clock on the mantelpiece in the kitchen. He had been losing heavily. Earlier that day men had come to the house and there had been a lot of loud talk in the bar. Emma hadn't heard what they said, she hadn't wanted to hear, but she had known it was nothing good, threats perhaps as to what they might do if he couldn't pay.

It had happened before, they had moved several times. Each time she hoped it would be the last, but it was never more than a year or two at most, and she should have grown used to it by now. She could remember as a small child being helped up on to a cart with their belongings in the dead of night, sometimes when it was cold and raining, being taken from a warm bed and wrapped up.

She realized now that she never thought of anywhere as home, it was just somewhere to live until things became bad and they must move on again. They had been in Cumbria at one time, near Carlisle, and then in the country around Penrith, and then in Northumberland, beside the sea, and a particularly difficult time once in the middle of Newcastle where there were big rats – or was it just her childhood nightmare, she could not remember – and then Durham, under the shadow of the great cathedral, a dwelling so ill favoured that it was never dry. Sometimes they stayed a few months. Their stay in Weardale had been one of the longest.

There was never enough to eat when she was little, and her most persistent memory always was of her father and mother fighting and her mother fearing there would be more babies, and then, after Margaret, her father had, in a drunken temper, pushed her mother down a short flight of steps, perhaps when

11

she was pregnant – Emma was too young at the time to remember – and after that there were no more children.

All her life she had wished they could get away, but to where? Her mother had no friends, even if her father had allowed it, there was never any time for such luxuries and she had no family that she had ever spoken of, so there was nothing but the getting by every day as best they could.

Josh had been everything to Emma. Now she felt as though he too was gone, as everything always was.

Her mother did not complain, she began to pack and they helped her, but she shed a few tears. Emma went to her father in the bar that very evening, before the rush started.

'Where are we going?' she asked.

'You'll know soon enough.'

'I think Mama should know.'

'So that you and she can shout it all over the village? I don't think so. The fewer people know we're leaving, the better, so keep quiet. You can help me in here tonight, your mother's got enough to do.'

Her mother was emptying her only decent china out of the corner cupboard.

'I don't want you in there, Emma,' she said when told.

'It'll be all right.'

When the time came, however, her father got hold of her and told her to loosen her hair and pull down the dress across her shoulders.

'The men like to see a pretty woman. God knows they don't see many,' her father said before he went in.

Emma did her best to secure the hair back to her head with the two pins which were still in it, and she pulled the dress to rights as best she could, hoping he wouldn't notice. She told herself that it wouldn't be too bad, and she supposed it wouldn't, but all she could think was that, when she wrote to Josh, she would not tell him that she was obliged to serve beer in order to get by.

The men told her how bonny she was, but nobody touched her, so Emma smiled and made brief replies and spent her entire evening wondering where they were going. No doubt her father had worked some scheme to get them out of there, and if they were going somewhere they could not be traced, it must be quite a long way from here.

She tried not to panic. All she had to do was to write to Josh and tell him her new address when she reached it, that was not difficult, and she had his address in Bristol.

Her real fear was that he would not come back. She told herself that this was ridiculous, he must come back, his family were here, but she knew that Methodist ministers and their families were moved on every three years. Perhaps he would not get her letters and they would go and she would never find him again.

She began to dream about it, to wake up with a cry because, in as many ways as her wretched imagination could devise, she lost Josh each night and would come round in panic in the half light. Lucy reassured her but she knew that it was just talk. Lucy was no more secure than she was.

That final night, when they lay in bed with the windows open, for it was full summer in the dale, she wished more than anything that Josh would come home and that they would not have to leave this place. Because of him, it held for her the happiest memories of her life, and now she was about to lose it.

She could hear the river from her window and thought of their final day together when they had stood in the middle of the bridge and he had told her that he loved her, that he would come back and they would be married. She must hang on to that memory, it had been the most significant and the most difficult day of her life. Whatever else happens, she told herself, I will always have the love of the best man in the world.

There was a part of her that believed it and a part of her that wanted to laugh over it, because nothing that good had ever happened to her before and maybe it never would again.

They didn't sleep. There was no point. As soon as it was as dark as it was going to get, the horse and cart arrived and the man helped her father on with their things. They set off into the night, down the dale, through the little villages of

13

Westgate and Eastgate, beyond Stanhope, the little town where the big limestone quarry was.

When it was daylight, they stopped and had something to eat. There was no kind of shelter but it didn't matter in such weather, and they moved on into Frosterley, where black marble was quarried, down past Wolsingham with its steel-works, following the twisting winding road which lay at the bottom of the narrow valley. She had hoped they would not be leaving the dale altogether.

Eventually they did, trudged up the steep hills, and she kept looking back, because all the countryside was spread out before her in its summer green and white.

When they got to the top of the hill, the dale was gone and the land was quite different. It was like emerging from a dream into reality. This was the countryside of the Durham coalfield, the beginning of it, the place where the finest coking coal was mined, and it was strewn with nasty little villages, the like of which she remembered only too well from having been through them before.

The pretty neat fields gave way to moorland, the streets straggled around pitheads. Dirty, ill-shod or barefoot children gazed as she paused, and it seemed to her that she would be on the road forever. Margaret cried with tiredness but her father would not let her sit on the cart. Rosamund was pale but said nothing and Lucy trudged along with her head down.

Eventually they reached a small town which seemed to Emma to be the middle of nowhere, and here, towards the end of the one main street, they turned up a narrow cobbled road and then left along an even narrower back street, and right at the far end stood a building quite alone. Here her father finally stopped and announced that this would be their new home. The sign outside proclaimed the building to be the Ivy Tree Hotel.

It must once have been a good building but it was neglected. There was a small overgrown garden to the front surrounded by iron railings.

A few doors along from it was the Primitive Methodist Chapel. That should have been funny or somehow appropriate, that the two worlds which were so important to her could exist there almost side by side, with only a few grubby little houses between them.

Too weary to look further about her or care, she began, under her father's instruction, to unload their belongings from the cart. They all helped. Inside, it smelled cold and damp and, although there were several rooms downstairs, they were cheerless, with fireplaces full of soot and feathers from dead birds, a kitchen where there was nothing but an old stone sink, but when Emma walked into the public room she was surprised. There was a piano and even a stage. Could the place have been some kind of music hall at one time? It certainly seemed so.

The piano still played. She lifted the lid and pressed a few keys and she heard her father in the doorway.

'It wants tuning,' he said, 'and then you can sing for the men.'

Emma didn't want to do anything of the kind, but she was too wise to say so.

'It's a nice big room,' she said.

'Aye, it's all right. I don't suppose the pitmen care for the state of it as long as there's beer and tobacco and a pretty lass who can hold a tune.'

'It's a pitmen's pub then, is it?'

'What did you think it was, the Savoy?' he said, laughing.

'How did you find it?'

'A little bird told me.'

Emma said nothing and he came further into the room and said in a halting tone, 'I used to live here, when I was a boy. I was born here.'

'You owned it?'

'My family did, once. They don't any more. The pit owner has it now.' He seemed reluctant to talk.

Emma was curious at his tone.

'Who is that?'

'Daniel Swinburne, Allan's son. The only way he could get an heir – and that was what he needed, him so clever and so rich – was by an Irish tinker's bitch. He couldn't marry her, of course, but he ended up living with her and the brat. I remember him as a little lad, nowt like his father, the living spit of Theresa MacGrath.' He laughed. It was an unusual sound and should have been nasty, like the rest of her father, but it wasn't. He always took deep pleasure in other people's misfortune, and enjoyment couldn't sound bad.

'It's a fine place, don't you think?' he said, turning full circle in the bar. 'I was always fond of it.'

Emma gazed around her. How strange to think that her family had lived here so many years ago. It was the first time that she had had any notion of a home, and there was a stupid sentimental part of her that was glad her father had, for whatever reason, decided to come back.

'My mother used to sing,' he said. 'She was like you, she had a voice.' And he wandered out of the room.

Her mother wept, but privately, when her father was in the bar late that night, drinking and presumably, Emma thought, thinking of better times.

'I never thought to be so low.'

'But it was the family place, surely.'

Her mother looked at her.

'Did his parents live here?'

Her mother looked wearily at her.

'They died a long time ago, and mine. I was never happy here.'

She didn't go on, and Emma was too wise to ask. Emma didn't need things explaining. Her mother hated being married to such a man, was ashamed of his drinking, his gambling, his uncouth ways, his . . . she hardly dared to think it, the way that he treated her mother. No woman should have to put up with being treated so badly. It was . . . what was the word . . . inhuman? It was unjust. It was . . . How had men ever thought of women in such ways? How very strange, how very threatened they must have felt to want to degrade the mother of their children. Was not marriage meant to be an equal thing? Why must women be made to hide? What was it that was so shameful? Was there ever real love between men and women? She thought she had found it with Josh but he was gone.

But why has he brought us back now, was the question she did not ask her mother.

16

She went back into the bar when it was very late and everything was still, and she pressed the piano keys and they responded, making what seemed to her a brave noise in the silence, and because the room was so big and empty, the notes echoed. Music could do things that words could not, she felt sure. If there was music there was hope.

The rest of the house was a possibility. Her mother didn't think so, she could see. It was bare, draughty, empty and their poor furniture did not fill a quarter of it. But Emma liked the space, whatever there was about it which was the essence of what had been, what was now and what would be – which was home – and she went to bed believing that she was beginning to understand why her father had come back to the place where he had been born. Perhaps he could not stand to be away from it any longer, though it was such an awful drab little pit village it would take somebody who had been born there to feel that way.

She went to bed, ignoring Lucy's sarcastic remarks – in her way, Lucy was as much like her father as Emma was. Emma could hear the wind across the fell and later when the rain came, even though it was cold and dark and she did not know what this place had to offer her, she went over in the depths of the night and opened the window.

Lucy was sleeping by then and there was nobody to see how foolish she was when she stuck her head out of the window the better to feel the cold drops. She had heard of wonderful places, of cities, London and Paris and Rome, but it seemed to her at that second that there was nothing better than this. You could taste the heather on the rain. You could remember the bees going about their business and the colour and the warmth and the way that the wind went hissing its way through the heather.

She left the window open and went back to bed and she lay down and rain licked its way around the building, this place which had been the house of her ancestry, she knew it, even though her father said little about it, and even though it was a humble place, with little land and less comfort, she saw it for hers.

Three

'My dearest Emma,' Josh wrote, and then thought it looked silly, but what could he put? Could he put 'My dear Emma'? Even that wouldn't do somehow. He couldn't remember what he had put on the first letter. Had she got it? She hadn't replied. Had she given him up so very soon? He couldn't think so. He wanted to tell her all about Bristol but he didn't want her to think he was having a good time without her, so how could he convey all that he saw without any enthusiasm, or would she worry more if she thought he was lost and homesick?

He was. He longed for the little dales town and her presence, and he wished he had not been so terribly righteous and stupid. He had thought at the time that he had to be, for both their sakes, now it just seemed ridiculous that, having the most beautiful girl in the world, he had barely touched her. He wanted her now more than anything.

He wanted to rush back and take her into his arms, run away with her and marry her and keep her safe forever from the dreadful man her father was, from anything that might hurt her. He wished she would write and tell him that she still belonged to him.

He hated Bristol, he hated the comfortable, almost luxurious, existence which he had somehow fallen into. Talking to the other young men who had come here to study for the same reason, they all seemed to be living or lodging in much poorer circumstances, he could not understand what he was doing with the Matthews family. They had been friends of his parents' friends and had offered. He had the feeling that if his parents had known how he was living, they would have disapproved very much.

Mr Matthews had even insisted, very politely but nonetheless firmly, that Josh should be taken to his tailor. He thought he looked absolutely awful in the new clothes which they had bought for him, not at all like himself, like somebody who thought he was too good to work, how ashamed his parents would be of him for living like this, but what was he to do?

The other young men had been taken to the homes of poor people, had been shown the other side of Bristol – the coalfields, the brickyards, but his life was a succession of dinner parties and social occasions where young ladies played pianos and sang and people talked of things which did not matter to him.

He hardly dared say anything, because Mr Matthews introduced him to people who had money and they were willing to spend it on worthy causes, but it was nothing like the kind of work he wanted to do, he seemed to get further and further away from the simplicity of his ideas about preaching and praying and being of some much more obvious use.

When he tried to express these views to Mr Matthews, Diarmud would smile and say that he understood, but there were all kinds of ways in which to accomplish good works, and money was not something to be despised when it could be put to good use. Josh was afraid that he had been ungrateful and offensive, so he studied hard, rose earlier, prayed often and did the best he could within the confines of the society he was allowed. It was a test, he decided, could he be corrupted to give up everything for comfort, luxury and ambition? Perhaps he could. Perhaps he was not the man he thought he was, or that his parents wanted him to be.

He grew to like Bristol. It was the city in which George Whitefield had started the first Methodist church. John and Charles Wesley had done all kinds of good things, setting up schools, and a college for young men like Josh, and beginning Sunday schools for children who had no other way of learning to read and write. There were some proper schools within the city now, but Josh could see that there was still a great deal to be done in the field of education, when small children worked in factories and mines.

Industry thrived here, cloth mills, tobacco, chocolate – the sugar trade from the West Indies. The harbours were thick with masts. Tobacco and molasses came through the docks. There were huge warehouses, soap factories, chocolate factories, and the coalfields of the northern Mendip. Textile mills made clothing from wool and silk and in the area around Bristol there were lace, tanneries and glove-making. Josh got to see a great deal of it, for he asked questions and got to know people, and they showed him everything in the area.

Quaker businessmen owned a great deal, and Diarmud Matthews was friendly with them, and when he was invited to their fashionable homes he took Josh with him. It was a long way, Josh thought, from the thorn tree under which Wesley had preached in the open air in Weardale, but here, just as at home, the liberty of the common people was sacrificed for money.

There were more masters and many of them were kind and wanted education and enlightenment for their workers, but he spent his free time in the narrow cobbled streets, the little Georgian shops, the lovely houses with their overhanging balconies.

Each day Josh would scour the long narrow hall table to see if there was a letter from Emma. Patience saw him there during the first week of his visit and smiled.

'Waiting for something in particular?' she said.

'Yes.'

Was the smile a trifle forced or was he vain? He thought Patience liked him but he didn't think she was interested in him. Why should she be? He would never be anything but a minister, and she knew a great many wealthy and influential men who would do much better in the world than he would, and she so obviously cared for things which should not have mattered, and he could not be reconciled to that. He always had to think hard and search his mind for something to say to her, and even then it always sounded stupid.

'She's called Emma Meikle. We're going to be married when I get home.'

*   *   *

Patience had not intended to pick up the letter addressed to him from the table. She could tell it was from a woman, perhaps his mother was writing to him, but somehow she thought it was not from his mother. As he approached, she slid the letter into the pocket of her dress, and now she did not know how to put it back on to the table without him seeing or somebody else noticing, and even after he had gone, her mother and then her father came into the hall in succession, and she had no opportunity to replace it.

She went up to dress for dinner and there she could not resist breaking the seal and opening it and she was astonished. The girl couldn't spell, she hardly knew how to put a sentence together; it was an awkward, uneducated letter. Patience could not think what he was doing with such a girl. Was she just the first that had caught his eye?

She wondered whether his parents knew, and doubted it. They would never have let him become involved with someone so unsophisticated. Worst of all, she gathered as she read, this girl actually lived in a public house. Was he mad?

She read it through twice and then decided that there was no way in which she could now put it back on the hall table, so, guilty as she felt, she put it on the fire. She then wished to confess what she had done, but she could not, and neither could she eat anything, so that her mother asked her if she was feeling unwell, and she took the opportunity to escape from the table and go upstairs, where she shed several tears over the young woman who was so devoid of any proper feeling that she stole a letter addressed to a young man whom she knew longed to go home, longed to hear anything from the girl he was undoubtedly in love with.

The trouble was that Joshua Castle had turned out to be something of a surprise to Patience. He was the only man she knew who cared nothing for ambition. He was eager to get back to whatever grubby little place he had come from, so that he could help people, and although she knew it was a laudable thing, she found that she liked him, she was in real danger of forming a substantial attachment, and he was the very last person she should have thought of.

21

Did it not occur to her parents that she liked him more than she should? Why would they think about it at all? He was so far beneath her. Eligible young men were plentiful in Bristol. Whatever could she possibly see in a boy from a Durham dales village? He had, though she hadn't found it in her heart to hate such a thing, a northern accent. He had no social graces, no real manners, he knew nothing of art or literature, he had no connections, had never travelled beyond Durham before in his life, but every time she wanted to think scornfully about him she couldn't do it somehow.

He did not want to create wealth or do good, he wanted a little chapel somewhere probably very obscure, and for that he would need a wife who could exist in such circumstances and no doubt bear him a number of children he would not be able to keep in any good form. It was not for her, and yet she longed for his presence, was bored with the friends she had cared for before he arrived, kept waiting to hear his warm soft voice from across the room. He would make a wonderful preacher, she thought, and without ambition it was such a waste.

Worst of all he didn't like her. He thought her empty-headed and overindulged, she knew, and that piqued her. He never talked to her freely. His conversation with her was stilted and awkward. No wonder her parents did not worry about the possibility of her falling in love with him, he had nothing to recommend him other than his brilliance as a speaker and his quiet, contained manner. He was socially below her and she was used to educated, rich young men, so it was a humbling experience to know that she could care for somebody like him.

The men she knew had good backgrounds, fine families, had travelled, read poetry, sent her flowers. Josh only spoke when he had something sensible to say, he didn't make conversation for the sake of wit or entertainment. She tried to be bored with him but she couldn't manage it.

All this was in her mind when she happened to be in the hall as the post came several days later, and with it another letter in the same hand. Patience was not going to take it from the pile but she did. It was not that she wished Emma Meikle – what a ghastly common name – any harm. Indeed, the girl was welcome to a man who would never amount to anything, but he had hurt her pride and she was determined now to make him fall in love with her.

Patience put the letter on the fire because it was ill-written, misspelt and blotted, probably with tears. How awful, to cry as you were writing a letter. It said nothing intelligent or interesting and worst of all pleaded with him to come back.

There was nothing to be gained by his seeing it, Patience decided, he could not go back, so it would only make his life worse, and things were bad enough. He was pale, did not eat much, had lost weight, and while Patience was quite sure that he would stay for those two years, because it was what he had set out to do, what his parents no doubt wanted for him, she knew that he was homesick. Patience was ready to wash her hands of him, to be content with more outgoing young men. They were all better than he was in every possible respect. She would punish him for thinking himself so superior. It would serve him right and then she would learn to despise him for his stupidity.

Josh couldn't understand why Emma didn't write to him. Had something gone wrong? His fevered imagination gave him all manner of disasters. Or was it just that she hated his absence and resented it so much that she had forsaken him for someone who was actually there? It wasn't difficult to believe. He didn't know what he was doing here. He wasn't doing any good, that was obvious to him.

He had come to feel impatient to be gone from the elegant streets, the flowing Avon, the shops with goods which people didn't really need, the bustling quays, the crowded docks, the streets where trees grew amongst the paving stones. He should never have come here, it was nothing to do with him. He studied very hard and paid a great deal of attention. The rest of the time he tried to be polite to the Matthews family and their friends while he waited in vain for a letter from Emma.

His letters from his family all came, and he longed to ask

them for news of her, and then he felt bad, since he had not told any of them, not even Wes, that he was in love with the publican's daughter. He was ashamed of it and ashamed of not being open and taking the consequences of his actions. Something had gone wrong and he did not understand what was happening.

Four

Langley Colliery was a thriving frontier town with an iron and steelworks, several pits, a brickworks and various industries linked to all those things. It had a railway which ran to Bishop Auckland and Durham and Darlington, and from there to Scotland and to London. It had two chapels, the Primitive Methodists and the Wesleyan Methodists. The Wesleyan Methodists' chapel was on the main street. Then there was the Presbyterian church at the top of the main street, the Catholic church on the corner where the road ran towards the Delight pit, its pit rows, and further on to the fell, and the parish church which stood on the front street with a long path up to it and plenty of room for the local people to visit the graves of their families.

There were lots of shops and houses, a national school in Smith Street, a mechanics institute where the men went to play billiards and talk, and there were forty inns and beer houses. It made for lively Saturday nights.

Just beyond the town, Allan Swinburne and some other men who made up the Deerness Iron Company had taken possession of the royalties of coal and sank a shaft which they called the Delight. It was the largest pit in the area now, and although Allan Swinburne had died some time back, his son Daniel ran the pits and the ironworks.

Emma's father insisted she should wait on and he had been right, it was a pitman's pub, the first place the miners passed on their way from the Delight.

They came covered in coal dust, their blue or brown eyes deeper-coloured within their black faces. Their accents were like a foreign language to her, they did not speak like the

25

people in the dale, they had thick gutteral voices, a patois all of their own, and they talked rapidly, so that unless she listened very carefully she understood nothing.

They called her 'pet', and some of the young miners looked approvingly at her, but they were as careful of her as the farmers and quarrymen had been. She began to distinguish one from another, and in particular two friends who came in often, who respectfully called her 'Miss Meikle'. They were hewers, well paid, and they spent a lot of money in the Ivy Tree Hotel, since neither of them had any family.

Alec Wyness told her he lived with his grandma, and Brendan Kinnear, who drank more than anybody she had ever seen, lodged with people in the village. They came in almost every night.

And then abruptly Alec stopped coming, and when Emma enquired after him, Brendan pursed his lips together, shook his head and said, 'He's courtin' a chapel lass. She told him she wouldn't have owt more to do with him if he didn't give up the drink.'

Emma thought about Josh the more when Brendan said this. How simple when one of you could give something up and make everything right. She wondered what manner of girl 'the chapel lass' was.

Emma was lonely. There was not a single letter from Josh after she moved, so that she wrote again with her address, and as the autumn days became cool and short and dark, it seemed that there was nothing for her but work, either in the house or dealing with the miners. Her father was so drunk every night that often he could not manage the stairs and lay on the rug by the dying fire or on the old sofa.

She could feel the relief coming off her mother when this happened. Emma wondered what it was like to lie night after night by a drunk, smelling his breath, listening to his snores or, even worse, having him touch you. She remembered the kiss that Josh had given her and wondered if her mother had ever felt like that about her father.

Her father's drinking and gambling soon became known and they had no friends. One or two of the young miners asked Emma to go for a walk with them but she would have nothing to do with any of those who came to the pub. She saw no one else. The shopping was mostly delivered.

The odd time Emma ventured out on those wet autumn days, nobody spoke to her. Her mother did not even go to church. Sometimes in the evenings Emma would watch the Methodists as they went to chapel. There seemed to be a different activity each evening, and on Sundays the children went to Sunday school.

Emma liked the look of the chapel, with its big bold steps up to the front door and its long, wide, evenly spaced windows, set high so that it looked out over the moorland beyond the houses. She wished she could have gone there but, as the publican's daughter, she felt she was welcome nowhere.

It was a cold hard winter. Her father, as though he had not degraded himself sufficiently already, drank himself into a stupor each night, and he had already lost money. She caught glimpses of the man he might have been, making jokes with the customers. He was witty, clever, funny, but he ignored her sisters and only spoke to Emma because she helped him with the work. She wondered whether part of it was his disappointment in not having a son. He was always cursing her mother for having given him four daughters, as though it was all her fault and nothing to do with him. Men were strange that way.

One cold December night when the others had finished clearing up and she thought he had long since gone to bed, she found him in the back yard, not doing anything, just standing, and she realized for the first time that he was the person she had got her good looks from. He must have been a handsome young man when her mother met him.

As he heard her, he turned on her her own blue eyes, and in the light which spilled from the room across the yard he said, 'You finished?'

'Yes, Father.'

He reached out and touched her cheek and it was the first time she could remember that he had offered any kind of endearment.

'Go to bed.'

'Are you all right?'

'I'll be in in a minute,' he said.

Emma went wearily inside. The house was cold, the fires long since having died, except in the bar, and that too was now black in the grate. She did not linger, she hurried upstairs and into the big room she shared with Lucy, who had not long since gone up and was complaining at the lack of heat.

Emma quickly undressed, putting on a thick nightdress, a nightcap and socks before climbing into bed. Lucy was warm by comparison, but she complained about how cold Emma was, so she huddled in her part of the bed, trying to think of something nice.

'We won't be here much longer,' Lucy said.

'What do you mean?'

'Father owes money all over town, and Mother told me tonight that the rent on this place hasn't been paid since we got here, even though they've tried several times to collect it. We can't get anything more from the shops. What are we going to do?'

'He's drinking more now than he's ever done, so that costs, and some men came in tonight and he gave them free drinks, so they must be people he owes money to,' Emma said.

'Wherever shall we go in this weather?'

'There was a letter came this morning, and he wouldn't let Mother see it, but she thinks it was our notice to get out. She said it looked official.'

'I'm never going near a man,' Lucy said. 'I have the feeling they all end up like Father, and that all married women end up like Mother.'

'Then what will you do?' Emma said, glad to talk of something other than their troubles.

'I think a corner shop would be nice. I shall sell sweets to the children and have everything in tins, so that I don't have to scrape any vegetables or make any meals or clear up after any children. I will have a cat and sit over the fire and be an old maid.'

'It sounds wonderful,' Emma said, and finally she was warm

28

enough to turn over and sleep, thinking that she might end up in a corner shop. She had not had a single letter from Josh since she had moved, and he must have her address, because she had written several times before she gave up. Each time she found another way to excuse him, but all she had thought for the last weeks was that he had another girl and had been too much of a coward to tell her.

It was hardly surprising. He must know that his parents would not approve, that if he were to come home he should do it under different circumstances. Emma had seen how impulsive young men were by now, and she thought that Josh's declaration of love and how he asked her to wait, telling her they would be married, was nothing more than words.

Also, she resented that he left her here to lead such a life. If you loved people, you didn't do that. She tried not to think about what would happen next. She could not bear the thought of having to move again. She thought about Josh's God and whether he might grant her a single wish, and since she had never asked anything of him before, she put in a quick prayer just before she fell off the cliff of sleep, that they should not have to go, that they might stay here, even though it was an awful little town, just because it was somewhere to call home.

Five

Brendan Kinnear had been in love with Elizabeth Forrest all their lives. He could remember as a small grubby child wishing he could follow her about. She had lived in the next street from his. It was only one street in fact, but in other ways it was a different life. She lived on the front street and he lived on the street behind, and all of his neighbours were Catholics, and Elizabeth's neighbours were the more prosperous shopkeepers and small business people, and they tended to go to the Methodist church or the Church of England church on Sundays.

Brendan didn't go anywhere. He lived with a family who were not his, and he earned a living. He could not read or write and he had started as a small child down the pit and been there ever since.

Elizabeth could read and write and he had no doubt she could do lots of other things too. Her mother sold women's clothing. They lived above the shop and Brendan imagined it was a comfortable living. Elizabeth was always well dressed. She wore pretty hats and gloves and had new shoes, and when she was a little girl she always had new clothes for Easter.

He had never had new clothes, because he had always lived with the Murphy family and there were so many of them that there was never enough money for anything. He could have moved out, of course, but he didn't know how to, and as he grew older he paid his lodging and kept the rest for himself, and nobody complained, so it suited him. He went to work each day and he got drunk each night, at least when he was on the shift which allowed him to do so.

On Sundays he slept all day and Mrs Murphy made a huge

dinner. She was very good at making dinners. Brendan had nothing to complain about with the food, and she tried to keep the house right, but because there were lots of them, there was always somebody in bed, and she struggled to keep clean clothes on them all, because they went through so much.

Mr Murphy was a quarryman and worked at the sharp-sand quarry just out of the town. He didn't make a lot of money and he was a drinker too. Two of the three sons worked with him. The third had gone away somewhere, nobody knew, and the three daughters who lived at home all helped their mother. There were another two daughters, who were married and very often turned up with various offspring, so many of them that Brendan could not remember their names. They all drank. Even the girls and their mother were keen on beer, gin, anything they could afford, but it meant that they were not prosperous. Brendan didn't care. As long as he had enough to eat and drink, a bed to go to and friends, he was happy.

Alec Wyness was his best friend. He had known Alec all his life too. Brendan thought they were friends partly because neither of them had any parents. Alec had a very nice grandma and Brendan was in the habit of going to see Alec's granny any time he got tired of the Murphys, or when there were so many of them at home that there was nowhere to sit, which was frequent during the cold weather.

That December he and Alec sat over Granny Wyness's kitchen fire and smoked and drank beer before they went out, and sometimes after they came back. Alec's granny never told them not to. He thought she would rather they had not drunk so much, but since Alec tipped up his pay and was keeping them both, she did not complain.

They had a house all to themselves, because he was a hewer at the Delight, and Brendan knew Alec's granny was glad of it. Where would she have gone otherwise, if she had had no grandson to keep and look after her. Alec was a good lad, he brought in the coal, bought her pretty things from the market, supported them and still had enough for beer most nights.

Brendan had never thought that Alec was interested in

Elizabeth. Most of the lads in the village had asked her to go out with them in the evenings, but as far as he knew, she had always said no. Somehow Alec got her to agree. When he told Brendan, on a cold night in the Ivy Tree Hotel, Brendan found that he could not smile or say how nice that was for both of them, and that was when he knew that he loved Elizabeth, that he had always loved her.

He tried to hide his feelings, it was not as if she would ever look his way, and Alec was a canny-looking lad. No wonder Elizabeth had agreed, whereas he was nothing at all to look at, being big and ungainly and dark-featured. Alec stopped coming to the pub straight away.

Brendan was astonished. He was also jealous, not only that Alec was going out with Elizabeth, but also that Elizabeth had taken Alec's friendship, his company, away. He was lonely. He had other miners to talk to but they did not have Alec's conversation, and as the winter went on, Brendan drank more and more, he was so upset.

He went to see Alec's granny but the trouble with that was that she went on and on about how nice Elizabeth was and how she hoped Alec would marry the lass and settle down and how they would be able to live with her and what a much better lad Alec was since he had started seeing her. Granny Wyness looked years younger, her face shone.

Brendan felt as though the only good thing in his life was finished.

'You could stop drinking and come to chapel,' Alec said to him several weeks after he and Elizabeth had first gone out.

'Don't be soft.'

'I'm not. There are good people at the chapel and the minister's a nice man. He's leaving shortly, they're getting a new one. It'll be a shame. I don't think anybody could be better. Try it.'

'No, thanks.'

Alec looked seriously at him.

'Have you never thought about what will happen to you when you die?'

Brendan had thought a great deal about it and it did not make for comfortable thinking.

'You'll go to hell if you aren't saved,' Alec said.

'I am saved. I'm a Catholic.' This was meant to be funny, but for once Alec didn't laugh.

'I'm going to ask her to marry me. Will you come to the wedding?'

Brendan made the sort of positive noises he felt sure his friend would appreciate, and Alec was so much in love that he did not see through the pretence. Brendan was generous enough to hope that Elizabeth would say yes, but his heart grieved over it and over the rest of his life, which he did not seem able to put right.

At work, Alec was all smiles. She had agreed to marry him. Theirs was to be the first wedding that the new minister would perform, and though it was a shame that the other man was going, Alec could not help but feel that it was a new beginning for them all.

It was certainly a new beginning for Brendan, who ended up bedding a whore who lived on the edge of the village, drunk, crying, hating himself every second of it. He thought he was the foulest creature on God's earth, wishing, hoping, that she would miraculously turn into Elizabeth Forrest, and the tiny cold house with its sheets that smelled of too many men would be lavender-scented, her body his only. He thought of what it must be like on the first night of your marriage with a woman who had been with no other man.

It was so amazing that he could not imagine what it would be like to have a pure body, soft and sweet and all your own, someone who cared for you and was giving herself to you after a proper ceremony, so that people approved. A wedding must be a great thing when it was yours and you were happy.

How wonderful to have a baby who looked like Elizabeth, to come back from the pit to a clean house and the smell of baking and the brasses shining and Elizabeth standing in the doorway with a child in her arms and a smile on her lips, the water ready for washing and the dinner ready for serving.

He could not believe there were men who had so much.

Who deserved such happiness? He certainly didn't. He staggered back to the Murphy household, and there the lads kidded him about Dirty Bertha, the village whore. The woman that every man rode. They had seen him go there, they knew, they had all had her.

Euan, the youngest of them, was the only one who saw that he was sorry.

'It's nowt, Brendan, it's just the way things are. God doesn't care, you know. He doesn't give a shit whether you bed Bertha.'

And Brendan could not help wondering why God gave Elizabeth to Alec, but only Bertha to him, why some people had everything and other people were scrambling around in the muck and the mud and getting nothing but a mouthful of dirt. He resented it and he hated God and he cursed the Almighty's name. But it was only drink, it was only drink and Bertha's fat thighs and the way that he could not control himself.

The work too went on and on. There was no relief. There was no going home to a woman who cared or her sweet lips. There was no child, no home, no comfort, only Mrs Murphy with her dinners and the way that she tried. She smiled on him and he paid her and thought, yes, you earned, you paid for things, you could rely on money and work. All you could do was to pay your way. There was nothing else for him.

Was it something he had done? Was it something his mother or his father had done? Somewhere the debt was owing and he was paying for it now, in silence and in drudgery and in loneliness and in all the things which he could not help, the drink and the wanting to be better but not managing it. How did people get by without it? He could not think. It was all there was left, at the end of the day. No Elizabeth, no conversation, but he liked the pub. He liked the Ivy Tree Hotel and the pretty way that Emma Meikle always smiled and was always the same. Drink and Emma, you could rely on that.

Six

Alec had met Elizabeth Forrest in the women's clothing shop that she ran with her mother, one cold rainy Saturday afternoon. Alec had never been into such a place before, but his grandma was paying so much a fortnight to Mrs Forrest for various items of clothing – Alec didn't enquire too closely – and the woman who lived next door went to pay for them, since Alec's granny couldn't walk that far.

'Mrs Harries is poorly and I've nobody else to ask. Will you go?' she said.

'Can't it wait until next fortnight?' Alec had a horror of shops like that.

'It wouldn't be right. Mrs Forrest would think I couldn't pay.'

In the end Alec went. Mrs Forrest was well known in the village as the kind of woman who would have nothing to do with men. Alec paused before he walked into the gloom, stepping down, trying not to look around at things he knew nothing about.

The shop was empty and, instead of sour-faced Mrs Forrest, a girl stood behind the counter. She was small and slight and you wouldn't have said she was beautiful but she was neat, her hair was smooth and shiny and her clothes were a perfect fit. She had dark eyes which slanted upwards at the corners, and cheekbones which made her whole face look slender and fine-boned, and best of all, she had the kind of mouth which made him wonder what she was like to kiss.

It was as simple as that. Alec knew nothing of women, but the moment he saw her he wanted to marry her. It was so strange and so wonderful that he couldn't speak. She tried to do what the older woman would have done, he thought, smile politely but coolly and ask whether she could help. Alec explained his errand and she accepted the money and that was all.

He was back outside in five minutes but he made sure he went the following fortnight and he had prepared a little speech, during which he asked her whether she would go to a dance with him which happened to be taking place that evening.

She looked amazed and then she said, 'That's very kind of you, Mr Wyness, but I don't dance.'

Alec had never heard of a woman who didn't dance.

'I could show you,' he said, as though he knew about dancing.

'No, no, I don't. I'm a Methodist.'

'Oh,' was all Alec could think to say, and then, 'Mebbe we could do something else.'

She didn't say anything, she just looked at him.

Alec suddenly wanted to be anywhere other than in the shop, making a fool of himself in front of this girl who so obviously didn't like him. He tried to get himself out of the shop without any further ado, and then he turned around and bashed into something and ended up covered in hats and confusion. To make things worse, she started to laugh.

'I'm glad you think it's funny,' he said as she rescued him. 'I'll never come back here, even if me granny owes you money, until kingdom come.' And he got up.

'You look a treat in pink,' she said.

Alec didn't answer. His face burned so much it hurt.

'What's your name?' she said as they got up.

'Alec Wyness.'

'I'm Elizabeth. I close the shop at five.'

Elizabeth Forrest was not in the habit of lying to her mother, so even though she knew her mother would not approve, she put on coat, hat and gloves and announced before she left, 'I'm going for a walk with Alec Wyness. I won't be long.'

Her mother, a small, fat woman – Elizabeth hoped she

wasn't going to look like that when she was forty – stared.

'I've got the tea ready,' she said, indicating the well-laid table.

'It's just cold, isn't it? I'll have something later.'

'Isn't Mrs Wyness's grandson a pitman?'

'I haven't asked him,' Elizabeth said, exiting before her mother should go any further.

He was waiting for her at the end of the street.

'I've never done such a thing before,' she said as they set off walking down Ironworks Road, where the view of Weardale was bright with sunshine.

It had rained earlier and clouds so grey that they were almost purple threatened the sky. Elizabeth didn't care. She liked how bright and diamond-laden the hedgerows were, and how the lapwings hovered green and white overhead, shouting 'peewit' in alarm as she and Alec walked down past the iron and steel-works and rows of houses, out into the countryside at the bottom of the valley.

The rain began to fall in huge drops, and they sheltered under a tree and there Alec Wyness kissed her while the storm broke around them. Puddles filled the road, the stream in the gulley ran brown, and the black-backed horses in the field nearby shook their manes, heavy with water.

Elizabeth emerged from her first ever kiss entirely entranced. She said the only thing that might save her.

'Do you drink?'

'Aye. Does it bother you?'

'I think it might,' she managed.

'Kiss me again and I'll give it up. I'd give up the whole world for you.'

Elizabeth had thought that when you loved somebody, it would be a gradual, well-thought-out thing, but it was not. She fell in love with Alec there and then, as the raindrops fell on her upturned face and he put his hands on either side of her head in some kind of benediction.

They walked on and in a way she felt as though with each step, after he had taken hold of her hand, she was throwing all her cares and concerns away from her. She felt the relief surge through her body. She was not going to turn into her mother after all.

They stayed out until the light went, and even then she promised to see him the following day. When she got back, her mother was sitting over the fire.

'Wherever have you been?' she said.

'Nowhere,' Elizabeth said, floating upstairs to her room.

'What about your tea?'

'I'm not hungry.'

They spent the Sunday together and Elizabeth came back feeling rather guilty, with smarting lips and a triumphant feeling. Her mother had been on the verge of going to bed and came to her room.

'Whatever are you doing with that man?' she said.

Elizabeth was still wearing her outdoor things somehow, and stripped off her gloves.

'He's a nasty little pitman. I knew his parents—'

'I don't want to hear this,' Elizabeth said. 'I don't want to hear anything bad about him.'

'You cannot go on seeing him.'

'Why not?'

'He will . . . he will do awful things to you.'

Elizabeth was inclined to laugh but she didn't, for her mother's face was serious.

'I like him,' she said, 'better than I've ever liked anyone in my life.'

'He will hurt you and then he will leave you. Do you want a life like I've had?'

'I don't believe any two lives are the same,' Elizabeth said.

Alec Wyness would never leave her, he had already said so.

Seven

Emma's father called her into the bar one morning, long before they were due to open.

'I want you to go and talk to Daniel Swinburne,' he said.

'Talk to him?'

'Aye,' her father waved a letter at her. 'I had this from him. It's our notice to get out.'

Emma stared.

'Aren't we going?' she said.

'No, we're not.'

'But . . .'

'This is our house. You go to the foundry office and you talk him out of it.'

'Me?'

'Aye, you,' her father said, with a touch of amusement. 'Think you can do that, do you?'

'No.'

'Well, you're wrong.' He got hold of her and turned her towards the big spotted mirror which hung behind the bar. 'Look at yourself. He's just a common Irish bastard. You go there and talk nice to him. You tell him we haven't enough money but we'll pay him later.'

Her father fairly pushed her out of the door. Emma walked slowly through the town, horrified by the idea. Her steps faltered the nearer she got. She had never been to an iron foundry before and it was scary, the big buildings, the huge black iron gates, the men staring, whistling, making remarks to one another. One of them even shouted at her, so that she wanted to run, but she dared not go back.

At the side she could see windows with desks behind them,

so she went up the sandy path and inside. Nobody even looked up, and there were four men all busy. She went to the nearest.

'I need to see Mr Swinburne, please.'

He stopped and looked at her. He was quite old, older than her father.

'What for?'

'It's – it's business,' she said.

'You can tell me.'

'No. I – I have to see him.'

Another man got up from his desk and came over.

'Mr Swinburne won't see the likes of you, lass. What's it about?'

As he spoke, a tall, dark young man came into the office behind her.

'I want to see Mr Swinburne,' Emma said again. The words were almost choking her.

And the man behind her said very softly, 'I'm Daniel Swinburne.'

Emma turned around. He was tall, much younger than she had thought he would be, not much older than she was, but his blue eyes showed a cynical worldliness that sat oddly in his unlined face. He had black hair and pale, milky skin, very Irish-looking, her father had been right, but very good-looking, slender, wearing a suit like the other men in the office, though it was covered in dust, as though he had been at the works for several hours. His face and hands were grubby.

'Can I – can I talk to you?'

'I daresay,' he said, and led the way through the office and into a dark narrow passage beyond, and then into a small office. Neither he nor his surroundings were anything like Emma had imagined them. She had thought that he would talk differently than the local people, but he didn't, and that he would be obviously rich and refuse to see her, or look at her like a lot of the men did, eyeing her body, her breasts in particular, but he didn't do that either.

The office was untidy. Indeed, he had to move a lot of papers and put a chair nearby for her before she could sit down. It was almost dark in there, his office lay in the shadow of the

40

works buildings, and the short autumn day was never going to get out. As Emma sat there watching him and the window behind him, rain began to fall, blotting out everything. He sat down behind the desk and looked shrewdly at her.

'What can I do for you?' he said. He sounded tired, and as though only his politeness had got her there, or his curiosity. He didn't look curious or interested. He looked, Emma thought, despairing, as though he would be pleased to see the back of her.

'It's about the rent,' Emma said, and then couldn't go on.

'What rent?'

'For the Ivy Tree.'

He looked hard at her and, in the long silence which followed, Emma could barely sit still on her chair.

'And you are . . . ?' he said.

'Emma Meikle.'

There was another silence after this, during which, if she had had the use of her legs, she would have got up and run out of the office, but somehow she couldn't move. She thought frantically of something sensible to say, and only managed,

'We used to own it. My father was born there.'

'Is that right?'

'We need a little time to pay.'

'A little?' He laughed. 'Your father owes money all over the county, and beyond probably.'

'We have nothing,' Emma said, 'and I have three sisters. Just a little time. Please.'

After that he said slowly, 'How is your father?'

Emma shook her head and didn't reply, though she thought it was an odd thing to say, for, as far as she knew, they had never met.

Reckless and desperate now, because she could not go home and tell her father that she had failed, Emma said, 'If you put us out you won't hear me sing.'

'You sing?' he said, looking disconcerted, as well he might, she thought.

'I do, and I will sing for you. I will sing anything you like. Each night I will sing something new for you.'

41

It seemed to Emma that Daniel Swinburne went on looking at her forever.

'All right,' he said, finally. 'You can sing 'The Oak and the Ash and the Bonny Ivy Tree'.

'The same song every night?'

'Yes. At ten.'

'Will you be there?'

'Perhaps. But you can tell your father that I will require the rent and more, starting from next week.'

Emma did not tell her father about the arrangement, only that Daniel would wait another week and no longer, and her father laughed and called her a good girl. Emma hated that she wanted him to do so.

That night, amidst the smoke from the men's pipes, and the fire, the beer fumes and the dark shadows, she sang 'The Oak and the Ash and the Bonny Ivy Tree' and she thought she could see, in the gloom beside the door, Daniel Swinburne's tall figure. Her father had gone into the back for some reason, but as she sang, 'A north-country maid down to London had strayed, Although with her nature it did not agree, She wept and she sighed and she hung her head and cried, How I wish once again in the north I could be, For the oak and the ash and the bonny ivy tree, They flourish and grow in my north country,' he burst into the room, cursing, red-faced, far gone with drink and a look in his eyes such as she had never seen before.

'Goddamn you to hell and back, don't sing that!' he shouted in a hoarse, trembling voice, and when Emma had stopped and the old piano player's fingers were still on the keys and the room was silenced, Daniel Swinburne stepped into the light and he said, 'As long as you owe me money, I want that sung every night.'

'Danny,' her father said in a low, trembling voice, and Emma sensed here that she had unwittingly made mischief and Daniel Swinburne had let her. Her father could not even speak without his voice breaking, and as he stood there, she saw how old he looked, how defeated.

'Be careful, Shaun.' Daniel Swinburne eyed him narrowly.

'Or I'll put you on to the street and give you up to the constable, and then your family will starve.'

She couldn't stand the way that her father looked at Daniel, and it was not with hatred, it was with guilt, she thought, with shame. She went to her father and she said, 'It was my idea that I should sing for him to gain us a few days.'

'Aye, I know, lass,' he said, and she treasured the soft words from him.

Daniel Swinburne turned and walked out, and her father held her to him for the first time, as though he could not bear the emptiness in front of him.

Eight

Patience had never believed that she was good. She had pretended to herself that she was and gone on with her life, but she had not really believed it. The way that she behaved over Joshua Castle confirmed it. The trouble was that no matter how much she flirted or spent time doing good works at the chapel, Josh's behaviour towards her didn't alter. She looked at the pretty girl in her bedroom mirror – she did not believe she saw evil there, but neither did she see a girl who wanted for Josh what he wanted for himself. She had heard people say that if you loved someone you let them be who they were, you did not try to alter things, or manoeuvre anything to suit your purposes, you let things be as they would. She dismissed that as naïve. She even told herself that what she did was all to the good, since he could never have married such a girl as Emma Meikle.

She told herself that she would not go on burning the letters as they came, but somehow after the first it was difficult, after the second she did not mean to, but they came with such frequency and it was easier each time somehow. No doubt his letters were getting to her but every single one that came in Emma Meikle's cramped hand went on the fire, until she could do it without thinking, without feeling guilty or ashamed.

She didn't even read them, she just made certain that he didn't see them either. He would get over it, he would be a better person, he would be the kind of person who wished to marry a girl on his own level in so many ways, a girl on a higher level, so that he would become an important man. He must not be wasted, he must not go back to the obscure little

44

farm village and be lost. She would be the instrument of his career. She would be the making of him.

In time he would become happy and he would forget. In time it was true he stopped watching for the letters, but it was a good six months and more, and even then when he went past the hall table his eyes strayed to it as though some magic would conjure one of Emma's letters.

He grew silent and thin, refused any social gatherings and worked at his studies as she had seen no one work before. He would become a fine minister; he had, her father said, elements of brilliance, and even her parents muttered about how he must be helped, how he must not go back and be lost to a small circuit when he could do great things.

When Josh was obliged to go into company, she watched him as he talked to other girls, holding her breath sometimes and thinking he might find a wife there, but he never said much, he did not shine, he did not show to advantage, he was not charming or engaging, and as soon as he was allowed, he went back to his work and this girl and that told her how dull he was and she was glad.

Christmas came and went and she wondered for how much longer he was going to behave like this. Even her parents began to worry. Her mother told Josh he was not eating enough and her father called him into the study, and there, although Patience had just sufficient conscience not to listen at the door, she had no doubt her father spoke of his concern.

When Josh came out and went upstairs into his room and closed the door, she went after him, knocking softly, and when she didn't hear his voice she went in, not sure whether she would find him somehow dramatically upset for the first time, and there he was, sitting at his desk, calmly writing. He even smiled at her. That was the first time Patience admired him as a person and was so thoroughly ashamed of herself that she could not speak.

'Do you want to go home?' she said.

He answered shortly but evenly.

'I can't go home, I have to stay here. I can't disgrace my

family and the people who contributed such a lot to send me here.'

'But you don't like it?'

He hesitated.

'This is not the life for me.'

Patience was unwise enough to say, 'My father thinks you would make a great man—' and she knew she had made a mistake when he laughed shortly and said that great men were not made, and that he would be content to think he had done some good in the world, and that was when Patience knew something important, that all men were ordinary, which was what made the ones who knew it extraordinary.

'If you had influence and the ear of wealthy men, you could do great works, help a good many people—'

'Then I shall have to manage without. I lack the necessary skills to bend people to suit my purposes.'

She could have told him that he lacked nothing. Having him in the house had been enough to drive her beyond the bounds of what was right and proper. He had inspired her to do wrong. He had somehow made her lose control of what she had been brought up to believe, and go beyond her view of what was right. The truth of the matter was, she thought, that he was a very dangerous man, because, if he chose, he could make people do whatever he wished, and without his knowledge they would do deeds on his behalf. He was perhaps too young to see it, or was it that he had always known that power and tried to harness it for good, or was he of the kind of persuasion that made men so vain that they thought they saw God?

'Do you . . . is this what you wanted always?'

'The ministry?'

'Did God speak to you?'

He laughed, and for the first time in weeks the laughter hit his eyes and all the charm, all the likeability of him came back.

'I wish he would. How simple that would be.'

'Most men of your calling think he does.'

'Do they?'

'Perhaps you might be able to go home in the summer.'

He said he couldn't, and when she spoke to her father after she went downstairs, he looked grave and said he thought that if Josh was allowed to go home, he didn't think the boy would come back, that it would be a mistake to let him go now, when he was obviously unhappy. As the author of that unhappiness, Patience pleaded the case, but her father was unmoved. He would not even suggest it to Josh. It had cost a great deal of time, money, effort and perseverance to get him this far, and he must stay and see it through.

'He hasn't suggested otherwise. I believe, even given the opportunity, he would not. He's a better man than that. He wouldn't give up, but once at home . . . He will learn to make the best of it, like everybody else does. I thought you liked him. Are you trying to get rid of him?'

'I don't like to see him so unhappy.'

'He must manage. He does manage. He doesn't complain at all. I think you're worrying too much. It's kind in you, but I'm sure he'll be all right. It's less than eighteen months, no time.' Her father stopped and then said, 'I don't think we're the right people for him, that's most of the problem, but it will be part of his work to get on with many different kinds, so that's good for him too. You're a warm-hearted girl, my dear, to be so concerned about him.'

If he only knew, Patience thought, but she smiled and left her father to his study and his work.

After Christmas there were no more letters. She could only be relieved that the girl had given up. She would find herself a nice workman, marry and have babies and be happy. She could never have been the right wife for him, would only have undermined his good work and all the effort of everybody would have been for nothing.

As for Patience, when she went to chapel, she spoke to the minister there about how she could help, and though he looked surprised, he seemed pleased and even asked her if she would run one of the classes in the Sunday school. She could not wait to tell Josh, and his response was such that she was encouraged to go on and do more, to help with so much work at the chapel that her mother complained that she was out every night and had no time for more frivolous things.

This was her way to make up for what she had done, Patience thought. She would atone for her wrongs with good works. She enjoyed it. She even thought that the life of a minister's wife would not be so very bad, provided it was the right kind of place. Her father would no doubt find Josh somewhere just right and everything would work out.

Nine

Elizabeth did not know how to tell her mother that she had agreed to marry Alec. Her mother had done without a man for most of her life – she seemed to expect Elizabeth to do the same. They were barely speaking.

At first Elizabeth had told herself that none of it mattered, and her mother told her that it would not last, but she found that she could not let a day go by without seeing him, and she would make excuses and steal away from the shop at whatever time Alec was free.

Best of all, he took her to meet his grandma and Mrs Wyness was a generous loving woman who took Elizabeth into her arms in welcome and asked her to stay for tea. Alec's granny made bacon and egg pies with thin crusts, she pickled red cabbage and beetroot to eat with salad, she made jam, marmalade and jelly, she baked most days and her kitchen held the sweet scent of it and she smelled of sugar and raisins.

Elizabeth was lucky enough to have Sunday dinner there, and although her mother made what was supposed to be the same thing each Sunday, it had never tasted like this. The old lady cooked meat to perfection, covered vegetables in thick golden butter and salt, and her gravy was just the right consistency, neither too thick nor too thin. She made Durham salad – lettuce, onions, chopped finely, vinegar and salt and pepper, covered in cream to go with the beef. There were Yorkshire puddings which filled a whole baking tin, and sometimes she put parsnips under the beef to braise so they came out soft and caramel-coloured.

Tea was muffins or crumpets toasted by the fire, sponge cake fresh from the oven, endless cups of tea, and they always

49

used the front room on Sundays. Elizabeth liked nothing better than a cold wet day, sitting by Grandma Wyness's huge fire, toasting her face and the muffins, a long silver toasting fork held out well in front of her, the butter and raspberry and redcurrant jam waiting.

She put off telling her mother about Alec's proposal for a whole week, and every day he read her face and at the end of the week he said, 'You still haven't told her, have you? Are you ashamed of me?'

'It's not that.' She tried to turn away but he held her. They were sitting on the little bridge beside the stream a mile or so below the village. 'There's been just the two of us, almost for as long as I can remember.'

'You're a grown woman now, Beth.' He was the only person in the world who called her Beth. She loved to hear him say it.

That night she went home late. Her mother always waited up for her, and there, in the kitchen, Elizabeth told her.

'Alec's asked me to marry him and I've said yes.'

Her mother's face was almost mauve.

'You hardly know him and he's nothing but a little ginger-haired nothing. His father was a pitman and his mother was—'

'I don't want to hear what his mother was. They're both dead. All he has is his grandma and she's very nice.'

'Go ahead and marry him then, if you must, but don't think I'll be coming to the wedding, and you won't be living here. You can pack your things and get out.'

'You don't mean it?'

'If you like his grandma so much, you go and live with them.'

Her mother slammed away upstairs. Elizabeth could hear her crying and she knew what was required of her. She had done it a hundred times before. She must go upstairs and say that she was sorry, that she would not do it, that they would be together for always, only she didn't, not this time. She went upstairs to her own room and packed her clothes and her books and the one or two things which she considered hers, and then she walked to Alec's house, carrying all that stuff, and it was a long way, down the Store Bank and Grove Lane and on to the front street and past the station and up the bank until the street levelled, and then down the passage into the yard.

His granny opened the door. She looked surprised.

'Why, Elizabeth, come in,' she said.

Almost in tears, Elizabeth put down her heavy burdens. Her arms ached.

'Isn't Alec here?'

'He's at the chapel. Mr Finn wanted a piano moving or some such thing, and for some reason it wouldn't wait until the morning. Alec had forgotten about it, I think, and Mr Finn was here when he got back.'

'The organ. Yes, I do remember.' Elizabeth took a deep breath. 'Mrs Wyness, Alec asked me to marry him and my mother will have nothing more to do with me, and I'm sorry but . . .' She choked on tears there.

'Oh hinny, don't worry about it. Your mother will come round in time and until then you can stay here.'

'He told you we were getting married?'

'He asked me if I minded, as though you weren't the nicest lass in the world, and you would be coming to live here because it's a pit house. Otherwise we'd all have to go and live with your mother.' And Mrs Wyness pulled a face and made her laugh. 'Sit yourself down and I'll make you some tea. You'll have to sleep down here, but I daresay you won't mind that. It's the most comfortable bed in the house.'

Ten

Elizabeth Forrest and Alec Wyness were married in the January, only a few days after the new minister got there. Brendan had heard that he had come from up the dale, from a pretty country town. How strange it must seem to him, he thought, how different. It snowed and made the wedding prettier than ever.

Brendan had never been in a chapel before. Indeed, he was not into churches at all, though he thought he did remember the Catholic church being a great deal more ornate and entirely different, the sort of church where you felt obliged to be quiet, whereas here people were more inclined to make a noise, or perhaps that was not true, because he could remember chants, singing, joy, but he could not remember it with any degree of certainty, and he could not go to the Catholic church, just because he was not sure that he belonged. In truth, the only places he felt he belonged were Mrs Murphy's and the Delight pit.

The chapel was full of sunshine, that was his first impression, no stained glass, no dark corners, the windows, even on either side, upstairs and down – for there was an upstairs, and that had surprised him – let the sun or rain or whatever light there was from the moors spill over the whole of the building and fall wherever it would. He liked that. There was something about it which pleased whatever soul he thought he might possess, and it was little enough.

From the pulpit, the preacher could see everybody and everybody could hear him, it was like the heart of the chapel, and he would have been happy enough to be there but for the fact that Elizabeth was marrying Alec.

It was a good wedding, if there could be such a thing, and there was a gathering afterwards in the schoolroom next door, and there was lots to eat and drink, though Brendan could not but be conscious that there was no beer or whisky. He staggered off to the Ivy Tree Hotel. Emma Meikle provided beer and prettiness and conversation, no matter how drunk you became. He let the drink flow down his throat and he thought that there was not enough alcohol in the whole world to soak up his loneliness. Was life meant to be this way? Surely it was not. Surely everybody deserved a decent chance, a woman he loved who loved him, a house and a home.

It was ridiculous to think so, he knew. People were entitled to nothing. You could expect nothing. Some people got more. Some people got the whole world. When he was really drunk, when he had apologized to Emma in case he should offend her, though he could still walk and talk and smile and pretend, he left the Ivy Tree and it was snowing again, and Brendan thought that snow was different to different people.

To Elizabeth and Alec no doubt it was falling softly beyond the window as they kissed and held one another. What was it like to hold someone you loved so close? To him it was just an interval before he reached the Murphy household and there would be a dozen people and crying babies and arguing adults and singing, and to some people the snow was all the excitement that they would have, the weather something they could do nothing about, and on that night when he was alone and Elizabeth and Alec lay together, he knew that God favoured some people and did not care what happened to others, and it was the hardest lesson of his life. God had forsaken him and nothing in the world would save him. Nothing would end it or palliate it or help. Alec and Elizabeth had everything and always would, and he – he had nothing.

Eleven

Emma had been pleased that Alec asked her to the wedding. He came into the pub for the first time since he had begun courting Elizabeth, especially to say, 'You will come and see us wed. We want that very much.'

She didn't like to point out to him that she and Elizabeth had never met, so she couldn't want it, and that Elizabeth was very much against drink, so to ask the woman who helped run the Ivy Tree was not perhaps the most tactful thing he had ever done. She was glad to be asked but she tried to refuse. Alec would not have it. He wanted her there, so Emma agreed.

She was almost immediately sorry, because the new minister and his family moved in at Christmas, and to her horror they were Josh's family. She kept telling herself that they did not know about her, but it was difficult having them just a few doors up. Sometimes she thought she could hear the hymn-singing from the cold street, and sometimes she was convinced they heard her.

She thought she could sneak into the back of the chapel just before the service began and not be noticed. It was hard for her to watch other people's happiness. What had Elizabeth Forrest done to deserve such a nice man, the man she had chosen? The man Emma had chosen was two hundred miles away and she had not seen him in almost seven months. It was like a lifetime.

It was a pretty wedding. The groom never stopped smiling, the bride was radiant. The minister made such a good job of it, he had a most pleasing voice. Afterwards, when Emma would have run away, Brendan Kinnear came to her before she could move from the chapel, and said to her that she must come to the schoolroom and meet Elizabeth and join in the celebrations, and it seemed churlish to say no. She would have to go later, because she must open the pub, but for now she went with him.

He introduced her, but she could see that Elizabeth did not like her, or disliked her trade so much that it took her all her time to be civil. Emma was not used to being despised for something she could not help, and it stung. She wished she had stayed at home. Alec saw nothing but his pleasure at her being there, and Brendan hovered close by and said to her that if he didn't get a drink soon he would give up living.

Daniel Swinburne was there. Somehow it hadn't occurred to her that he might take part in anything in the village. He stood apart from other people. He was wearing a dark suit which made him look what he was – the pit owner. He looked back at her and Emma had not known she was staring, and turned away in confusion. And then, to her dismay, he came to her. She could not think why, and was aware of everybody in the room watching.

'Miss Meikle. Good afternoon.'

'I didn't think you would be here,' she said, and then wished she hadn't. It was a stupid, clumsy thing to say, but she had felt obliged to say something.

'Really, and why is that?' His voice was soft and he smiled.

'Well . . .' Emma said.

'Alec Wyness is one of my best workers, and Elizabeth Forrest is a lovely girl.'

Emma was still singing the same song every night at ten o'clock. Sometimes he was there, sometimes he wasn't, but it affected her father badly, even if he went outside or into the back. Standing there now, she found the courage to say, 'Don't you have another favourite song that I might sing for you?'

'What else would you like to sing for me, Emma?'

It was an impertinence for him to call her by her first name, as though she was worth nothing, and the way that he looked at her made the blood warm in Emma's cheeks, but she looked him in the eyes and said, 'Anything you like.'

'I like "The Oak and the Ash and the Bonny Ivy Tree".'

'Aren't you tired of it?' Emma asked wildly.

'Oh, I never grow tired of it. My mother used to sing me to sleep with that song. She had a pretty voice too, you see, though not quite as good as yours.'

'Why does my father hate the song so?'

'Why don't you ask him?'

'I wouldn't hurt him,' Emma said, and she walked out.

Her father was always drunk now, somehow more than he had ever been, night and morning he needed the alcohol. He was of no use in the bar. He no longer drank in a steady way with the men, laughing and joking and keeping the conversation in a steady flow such as he had always done. It had been his main talent, she thought. Now she ran the bar alone, did all the work, and very often he would not even come through, and she was obliged to ask Lucy to wait on, and to silence her mother's objections.

'I need the help,' she said.

'He's getting worse,' Lucy said when they were safely upstairs and the night was almost gone.

'I know.'

The only good thing about it was the fact that her father was never sober enough to count the money, and she was able to go up to the foundry office with it each week, but she went on singing for Daniel Swinburne because the debts were huge and they were obliged to stay where they were. Her father had come home and it was his last throw, she knew.

Twelve

Patience's mother seemed determined to keep Josh in Bristol.

'We should find a nice girl for him, then he would be much more content,' she said.

'The girls here are used to men with money and influence,' Patience said.

'Why, Patience, that's awful. I would think any girl would like Josh. He's a charming young man and not everyone cares for such worldly things. I'm surprised at you.'

Patience couldn't understand how the words had got out, they were not at all what she had intended to say. She had not thought her parents would have agreed to her saying that she liked Josh, but even if they did, he seemed to like her company no more than anyone else's, and that was not saying much. He saw less and less of other people. Was either out at lectures or in his room working.

Her mother was looking at her.

'The truth of the matter is that you love him, don't you?' she said softly.

'Yes.'

'Then why didn't you say so?'

'Because he doesn't care for me. He has a girl, or had, waiting for him, and I . . .'

'Oh Patience, how could any man not love you, you're such a wonderful girl,' her mother said. 'And you've done so much during the past months at the chapel, and . . . it was for him. You would make a perfect minister's wife, and if it is what you want, then we must do all we can to see it come to fruition.'

57

'Do you think so?'

'I see no obstacle. He doesn't look like a young man pining for the girl he left behind.'

'You don't mind that he doesn't have any money?'

Her mother looked at her in surprise.

'What gave you the impression I was that vulgar? I married your father because I liked him. He was beneath me, my parents didn't want it but they let me have my way, and I think it worked out very well, so I'm hardly the right person to tell you not to marry the man your instincts tell you is right for you.'

Josh certainly was not still pining for the girl he had left behind. He was, she thought, well past that stage. He thought Emma Meikle had given him up, perhaps betrayed him, grown impatient with his putting his own life before the life they might have together. Who could blame her for that? It was the truth. No wonder he regretted it, disliked his life here so much, but if he could form an attachment with someone like herself, it would improve everything so much.

Her mother planned a dinner party, but a small one, and she sat them side by side, and Patience had a new dress and her hair done in a new way, and her conversation could not have been more suited to such a young man. She could talk about all the activities which went on at the chapel, where she did so much work, and he was not rude enough to say he didn't care or wasn't interested. It was such a major part of his life that he had to be interested.

On her other side was Edward Johnson, the son of her parents' best friend, whose father was also in shipping. They were, if anything, wealthier than the Matthews family. Edward was a handsome young man who had gone into the family business, and Patience knew that, in spite of her mother appearing to be pleased that her daughter had fallen in love with a poor preacher, she would have been even more pleased should Patience have professed an attachment to Edward, whom she always referred to as 'such a dear boy'.

'So that's the preacher,' Edward said.

'I thought you'd been introduced.'

'I was late. He looks more like a poet. Very pretty.'

'Oh Edward, he does not.'

Edward looked sideways at her.

'Like that, is it? You can't marry him, Pat. He'll take you back to some disgusting northern hovel and buck you like a rabbit.'

Patience almost choked, and looked around in case anybody was listening, but luckily they weren't.

'Edward!' she said.

'You'll end up with half a dozen brats and not a decent pair of shoes to your name. Stay here and marry me.'

'Don't be ridiculous. You told me you would never marry.'

'I shall have to eventually. I'd rather you than anybody else. At least we get on.'

'And Clive?'

Clive was Edward's particular friend.

'Clive has gone off to South Africa to make his fortune. Unlike the rest of us, he didn't already have one about him.' Edward looked wistfully into the distance.

'Couldn't you have gone?'

'I'm the only son. Who would have helped my father to run the business? I couldn't leave. My parents would have been so disappointed in me. Let's get married, Pat. I can keep you lavishly and it would be such fun.'

After dinner, Edward talked to Josh for a long time and said to her when he left, 'Your northern boy is quite something.'

The other guests had all gone and her parents were not about. She went back to the drawing room, which she half-expected to find empty, but Josh was still there.

'What did you think of Edward?' she said.

'Are you going to marry him?'

'He told you, did he? He's always asking me. Do you think I should?' She watched him, biting her lip so that she shouldn't smile, pleased that he should take such an interest in her.

'I suppose that depends what you want from marriage.'

'Oh, very diplomatic,' Patience said. 'He thought you were pretty.'

Josh looked away from her and then said, 'He told me.'

'And what did you think of him?'

'I thought he was a lot more fun than most people. I liked him.'

'He's a darling.'

The moments passed while Josh didn't say anything, and then she was more surprised than she had ever been in her life when he took her into his arms and kissed her. Patience, aware of the open door and the possibility of her parents coming into the room at any second, pushed away from him and stood, wide-eyed, while he said, 'I've got this wrong, haven't I? You don't like me. I have become so fond of you and of everything here.' When she didn't say anything he went on, 'My parents are very poor. They give everything away. They're moving. I had a letter from my mother this morning. So when I do go home, it will be to some pit town and not the beautiful dales village.'

'Maybe you won't go home.'

'But I must,' he said. 'My whole life is there.'

'What if your life was here? What if there was something here so important that you didn't want to leave it?'

He looked at her and then he looked down.

'Is it a game?' he said.

'What?'

He looked up and it was a look so direct and honest that Patience was sorry for what she had said.

'You being nice to me. I don't know anything about women. Emma has been the only girl I cared for. I'm a fool, you see. I don't understand. When I try to kiss you, you won't let me. Lots of the young men who come here, they're in love with you, I can tell by the way that they look at you, and sometimes you encourage them, and when they are encouraged and fall in love, then you – you treat them badly.'

'You're impertinent!'

'Am I? I'm sorry. You're a long way above me, and I don't know how it works, but it seems to me that you like men to make fools of themselves over you, and I'm too poor to be able to do that and have any self-consequence left at all afterwards.'

'You do admire me then?'

'Well, yes, of course I do. Any man who ever met you couldn't help but be astonished at how beautiful you are, and you're so clever too, clever enough to take advantage of my stupidity and social inadequacies—'

'There is something special about you,' she said, and then stopped.

'What do you mean?'

'I don't know. Only that I can see it, and when women see that in men, they want to – to be a part of it. It's what I like best about you, that tremendous ability that you have. People listen to you, want to do what you want them to do. You remember everyone's name, ask after their families, all the details which nobody else can remember, like you care.'

'I do care.'

'About everybody?'

'Yes. It's . . .' He smiled. 'It's part of my job to care.'

'But you still have sufficient love left for – for the girl in Durham.'

He looked rueful and shook his head.

'I'm beginning to think that if I had cared for her as I should have, I would never have left. And now I think she gave up on me when I did, and I don't blame her for it. I put my own concerns before hers, and it's no way to treat someone you say you love.'

'Perhaps it wasn't meant to be.'

'I don't believe that. I think people can make their own lives.'

'Then why are many people so poor and wretched?'

'That's why I want to help, to make a difference, I want education for them so that their masters won't be able to dictate terms. Things could be a lot better. If they could be educated and band together, they could do a great deal to improve their lives. That's what I want for them.'

She had never heard him talk like this. Indeed, a lot of people she knew would have been horrified by it, but she found it exciting. Most of the young men she knew were so self-absorbed that they had no finer feelings, and this was what she had found wanting. Josh really thought he could make a difference to things, and she was beginning to think so too.

Thirteen

By the spring, Elizabeth was pregnant with her first child, and Alec went to work with a shining face. The other men teased him rudely and he was so pleased that he invited Brendan to the house for the first time. Brendan did and didn't want to go, but he went because he could not think of an excuse.

The little house was different than when Alec had lived there alone with his grandma. The old lady was more animated than ever, and it was so clean and tidy that Brendan hardly dared sit down. Elizabeth would not only not have drink, she did not approve of smoking either, and over the meal – the food was also perfect, something Brendan did not find difficult to bear – she said to him, 'You should come to chapel with us on Sunday.'

To Brendan's surprise, Alec said, 'He doesn't want to come to chapel, Beth. He's perfectly happy as he is.'

'I don't see how anybody could be, living that way, and you said yourself you were bothered about him.'

Brendan stopped eating the delicious steak and kidney pudding and said, 'What are you bothered about me for, Alec?'

When Alec didn't answer, his wife said, 'He doesn't want you to go to hell.'

Brendan looked at Elizabeth.

'I'm not going anywhere,' he said.

'You will,' Elizabeth said, and Brendan had to stifle a desire to push her face into the dish of mashed potatoes, which was sitting almost in front of her.

'I'm a Catholic,' he said.

'You don't go though, do you?'

'No, I brave God's fury.' Brendan was surprised at how the words came out, all neat and bitter.

Elizabeth looked at him.

'You're being funny at my expense,' she said.

'Sorry,' Brendan said, and ate his dinner.

The strange part was that he didn't dislike Elizabeth because of her narrow-mindedness. It didn't, unfortunately, stop him from thinking of all the deliciously dirty things he had always wanted to do to her. Perhaps that was the solution to everything, a mixture of fear, tight-knickered ideas and sin. Brendan didn't know. He didn't function terribly well without a drink by the middle of the evening.

She saw him out. Alec was attending to the old lady who needed help getting up the steep stairs.

'You'll be off to the pub then, eh?'

'Oh aye. Emma Meikle has the sweetest voice on God's earth.'

It was cold outside and a million stars were shining.

'She'll not be at the pub singing for much longer by what I gather.'

'What do you mean?'

'I hear Mr Swinburne has taken a fancy to her. He's always there. She sings for him, the same song all the time. Folk are talking about it. I don't suppose he'd marry a lass like that though, would he? He would more likely set her up in a little house on the edge of the village and keep her.'

Like Dirty Bertha, Brendan thought, and felt sick at the idea.

'I know nowt about it,' Brendan said, suddenly unwilling to betray either his employer or his friend. 'I'm so pleased for you about the baby.'

She shivered.

'I hope it'll be all right,' she said.

'I'm sure it will. You and Alec deserve to be happy.'

'I hope I haven't offended you,' Elizabeth said, and in a way he wished she hadn't been so nice to him, because he remembered then how much he loved her. She made it worse,

64

she kissed him on the cheek and the brush of her body destroyed his peace of mind.

'You couldn't offend me, love,' Brendan said, and he walked away.

Fourteen

That winter Josh received a series of letters from his brother Wes. It was as he suspected, they had moved from a lovely quiet village to the kind of frontier mining town which must have been an interesting place to live if you were a young miner with lots of friends, able to go drinking on Saturday nights.

Unfortunately, their father kept Wes at his studies and at home. They seemed determined that he too should be a minister. Josh doubted his brother had the temperament for it, though he took comfort in the thought that the threats posed by beer were nothing more.

There were other surprises. Wes reported that the Meikle family, who had left in the night without paying their bills, were running the pub just a few doors away. Mr Meikle had died and the men were flocking to the place because Emma had the most beautiful voice and she sang for them. Josh wished he had been there to hear her, and was envious of all the men who listened, and resented their presence, and that she had to sing in such circumstances.

Wes also said that the news in the village was that Daniel Swinburne, who owned the pits and the ironworks, went there often, people said he had never been taken with a girl before as he was taken with the beautiful Miss Meikle. He went to the Ivy Tree Hotel night after night to hear her sing. Josh wondered whether that was why she had stopped writing to him, she had met a better prospect. Her future was uncertain. Perhaps she had encouraged this man because she needed to feel secure. Josh knew what her father had been, that they had never had any money because he was so profligate. Perhaps she had to marry for money. Then he called himself a fool. Emma would never do such a thing.

It could be that she was realistic and did not see herself married to the minister. He didn't blame her for that. He was finding it difficult to remember who the minister was. Here he lived in luxury, and to his shame he liked it, he liked the warm fires in the bedrooms, the soft cloth his suits were made of, the good meals that were provided, and the company at dinner. He liked Patience and how pretty she was, he even liked the frivolous things about her. Sometimes he thought that what he liked best about her were the silly little things and not the work she so strenuously did for the church.

He had begun preaching, he had had contact with ministers in Kingswood, where the miners lived. He had thought it might remind him of home somehow, instead of which it made him long for the safety and security of the Matthews house. Josh thought he had been there too long, he was becoming accustomed to this life.

He liked the educated people he met, the way that people complimented him on his sermons and they took his ideas seriously and talked to him about them as though they were something real, but late at night or at three o'clock in the morning – what God could have invented three o'clock in the morning, it was unseemly – he saw himself then, in the darkness, as he really was, vain, self-seeking, failing in all the things he had thought he most wanted to do, and he knew then that it had been a mistake to leave Durham, that he should never have tried to be a minister, he was not the right person to do this, he was too shallow, too easily pleased, not sufficiently concerned with the problems of other people.

Why had he listened to his parents? It was, he admitted to himself in the depths of the night, because he had wanted to please them. In doing that, he had spoiled his life, lost Emma, and would be stuck forever with fat, self-satisfied people telling him how wonderful he was.

He couldn't sleep. He got out of bed and down on his knees and prayed that God should send him home, and then remembered that you were not meant to ask for things, at least not things like that, not things to please you, but only for the greater good. What greater good could there be in his going back to Durham? He was not worth a second of God's time. And he prayed most stupidly, 'Don't do what I want you to do for any reason of mine.' He feared God's betrayal, the easy way the Almighty made a joke of you, and why should He do that when men were so small, so stupid, so easily swayed? Had He no compassion? Had He no mercy? The trouble was that Josh did not believe God had these things. He would never have condemned men to such misery.

Josh thought back to the last day when he and Emma had leaned over the bridge, and how beautiful it had all been, and he thought that was what God did best. He had made this wonderful place, so wonderful that men did not want to die and leave it, so even that was not pure, even that held men in false thrall.

He was so tired by his thoughts that he went back to bed and, in spite of wanting to think more on such large issues, he fell asleep straight away and worried no more.

Fifteen

It seemed to Emma that she had been in bed a mere five minutes before she heard her mother's cry from below. She got out of bed and was across the icy oilcloth and down the steep stairs so fast that it was only when she came to a halt and saw her father on the kitchen floor that she knew she was awake and it was morning. Her mother was standing still, staring.

'Go for the doctor.'

'Mama—'

'Go for the doctor,' her mother said again, and that was when Emma knew that it was serious, because they were poor and the doctor was expensive. Emma put on coat and shoes and ran out of the door, trying to forget how still her father was, lying on the rug by the fire.

She had to run the whole length of the main street. The doctor's house was at the end, through gates amongst a lot of trees. It was early, but there were people about. She was conscious of them staring at her as she ran, her nightgown longer than her coat, her hair still plaited, her legs beginning to sting with cold because they were bare.

She ran down the short drive and hammered on the door. She had to do it three times before a woman, obviously a servant, answered the door. Emma didn't have time to speak, it must happen often.

'He'll not be a minute,' the woman said.

He was not much longer than that, pulling on his heavy coat as they walked. All Emma said was, 'It's my dad.' And he nodded.

When they reached the house, she wanted to wait outside

or turn and run, but she showed him into the kitchen and he ushered them all out except her mother, and then he closed the door. Margaret was crying. Rosamund went off back upstairs. Emma thought none of them knew what she was doing. Lucy hovered outside the kitchen door, and so she waited with her.

Lucy began to cry, and then the doctor came out and she could see by his face that things were not good, and it was strange. She thought she had known right from earlier that evening somehow that her father was going to become ill.

Emma could not help feeling that Daniel Swinburne had had something to do with her father's illness, and she ran up to the ironworks, burst straight through the men and down the narrow dark little corridor and into Daniel's office. He was sitting at his desk, as she always imagined him, working, surrounded by papers. She had admired it about him that he was able to run six pits and an ironworks all by himself. Now she didn't admire anything about him.

'My father has collapsed!' she shouted as two of the men from the main office began their apologies for letting her in. They stopped at her announcement, and the tears which she had tried hard to keep back. 'He's ill and you did it. The doctor seems to think he may not recover, and we had to put him to bed and now . . . and now . . .'

'Leave us, please,' Daniel said.

The men went out. The door closed.

'I did it?' Daniel looked at her. 'How did you work that out?'

'That song—'

'The first man ever to be brought down by a song.'

The tears ran unhindered down her face.

'I will never sing it again.'

The look on Daniel's face changed.

'Oh, yes, you will,' he said. 'You will sing it every night at the same time, as long as you wish to go on living at the Ivy Tree. I take it you do, if your father cannot be moved.'

Emma swallowed the rest of her tears.

'Why do you want me to sing it, and why does it have such

70

an effect on him?' When Daniel didn't answer she said, 'Do you wish him dead? Did he do something to you? He isn't a good man, but surely it's years and years since he was here. Wasn't your own father unkind? He told me.'

'What did he tell you?'

'That your mother was an Irish tinker's daughter and that your father couldn't marry her because she was so low, but he ended up having you to live with him.'

'We lived in the kitchen,' Daniel said, and after that Emma wished that she had not been so cruel, the silence was so big.

'All right,' she said. 'I will go on singing the song for you every night, but I blame you for this.' And she turned and made her way out of the office.

She comforted herself. Josh would come home soon and they would be married and after that everything would be all right.

Sixteen

In the October, Brendan reported that Elizabeth Wyness had given birth to a little boy. Emma, who didn't pride herself on her knitting, had managed to make a nice little jacket for the baby and duly sent it round with a note, saying how pleased they were. The result was that one morning shortly afterwards, when Emma was washing the floor in the bar, Lucy came in, saying in whispers, 'Elizabeth Wyness is here. She's brought the baby.'

Emma had not expected any such thing, but she went through into the back room to find her mother with the baby in her arms, Margaret making tea and Elizabeth, pale but radiant somehow, sitting over the fire.

Emma had never held a baby, but when she did, it occurred to her once again how lucky Elizabeth was and how difficult therefore it was to like her. Now, however, Elizabeth was all smiles and thanked them so prettily for the present that Emma was drawn to her for the first time. Elizabeth was so obviously content with marriage and spoke warmly and affectionately about her husband.

Emma never saw Alec. She saw Brendan every night he was on the shifts which allowed him to drink in the evenings, but he was not drinking as much as he had been.

'Mr Swinburne threatened to get rid of me if I didn't cut down,' Brendan had said.

She asked Elizabeth about Brendan.

'We don't see him. I have so much to do, what with Alec on different shifts all the time and the baby to see to, and Alec's grandma isn't well, so I have to look after her too. There isn't time for other people.'

72

'He's very fond of you all.'

'Yes, I know,' Elizabeth said, and Emma thought, she knows how Brendan feels about her and yet, even married and with a child, she doesn't feel safe enough to allow him into the house, even though Brendan is the kindest and gentlest of men.

He sometimes drank with other people, but more often he would sit night after night in the Ivy Tree and listen to Emma singing. In a way, she relied on him to be there, and she would sing for him because Brendan was safely in love with another woman and they were friends.

Seventeen

That winter Josh did not have a letter from his father all through January. His father had been his most regular correspondent and the one person who made him try to get things right. Both his parents were sticklers for trying hard, but his mother had the other two boys to deal with, so she was not as nice in her requirements. It was a shock therefore in February to receive a letter from his mother saying how concerned she was about his father's health.

The doctor thought it was his heart. She had not liked to tell Josh, and had sworn Wes to secrecy, but their father had collapsed two days after Christmas and they had feared for his life. She did not think Josh should come home, since his father was getting better, he must stay there and pursue his studies, it was his father's dearest wish—

Josh stopped reading there. He went down to the study, where Mr Matthews was working. It was early evening and both of them had just come in. Diarmud greeted him as he always did, with a smile, and it occurred to Josh for the first time that Diarmud really liked him, as only a man who had no son could admire another man's child. Diarmud had long been calling him 'my dear boy', and, as a term of affection, Josh did not think it could be bettered. He spilled out the problem to Diarmud.

'My first inclination is to go home.'

'You mustn't do that. In another three months you will be ordained.'

'What if he dies when I'm not there?'

'Didn't you come here, in great part, because he wanted you to?'

'I can't do this any more!'

A shocked silence followed. Josh was ashamed.

'I'm sorry, sir, I didn't mean to be disrespectful,' he said.

'You're not being disrespectful. Sit down.' Diarmud spoke gently, and when Josh had sat, he got up and went over to the cupboard behind him and he took out a glass and poured brown liquid into it and handed the glass to Josh.

'Drink it.'

'What is it?'

'Brandy.'

Josh almost laughed.

'I can't drink that.'

'It's for the shock. Go on, it'll do you good.'

Josh did. It was warm, sweet, and had a heavy kick that made him cough slightly, just like medicine.

'If your mother had wanted you to go home, she would have said so,' Diarmud said.

'You've been very kind to me, but I'm finding it all so very hard. I wasn't born to be a gentleman.'

'You were born to preach. Everybody who's heard you knows it. You inspire people to do better things. It's a gift. You cannot give it up now. Believe that your father will get better.'

Josh tried but found himself standing in the gloom of the hall some time later, wanting to cry as he hadn't since he was a small child. There Patience found him.

'Father told me your father has been ill. I'm so sorry.'

All Josh wanted to say was, *I want to go home*, but he couldn't, and neither could he manage anything else.

After that he thought if his father was ill he would not be able to continue his work and the family would lose their home and everything. It was all the more reason for him to finish his studies, because if his father died he would have to look after his family. This was the only thing he would be qualified for. He must stay here and do it.

He thanked Patience and excused himself and went upstairs. He must work harder than ever. He must not fail.

In the depths of the night, however, he could not sleep. He

could not bear this room where he spent so many hours trying to shut out the social round which the Matthews family considered part of their lives. He felt stifled even though the fire had died and the room was cold. He stumbled downstairs in the darkness and huddled there in the warmest room, the sitting room, and then he wished he hadn't.

He imagined his father dying and he not being there to say goodbye, and how he had not really wanted to come here and how the cost had been so huge.

There was a flicker of light, a sudden small noise, and Patience appeared, a candle in one hand, her hair loose. She was wearing a long white nightgown with a shawl across her shoulders, and other than that looked like a child. She came in, closing the door carefully behind her for the draught.

'Are you all right?' she said softly, and she came and sat down beside him on the big sofa. 'Are you worried?'

'What if he dies?' Josh said.

'Your mother wrote because he was getting better, didn't she? My father said—'

'Yes, I know. What if it isn't true? What if . . .' He got up. 'I go preaching on about heaven. The truth is that I don't know anything about it.'

'Your father's been a good man.'

'I don't think he's any better than anybody else. Being a minister doesn't automatically make you good, and besides . . . oh, I can't remember the argument. I just miss him, that's all, and . . . I don't know what I'm doing here. I don't think I ever did.'

In the silence, Josh wished he hadn't spoken, or that he had said less, or that he had said something different. Patience said, 'My father had been hoping you would stay afterwards and—'

'This is not for me.'

'But I can't do without you,' she said, and he was surprised, listening as her voice wobbled.

He looked at her. It was difficult to see anything by the tiny light of one candle. He was surprised and rather pleased. She sat there, hiding behind a curtain of golden hair, and he

76

realized then that he would miss her too. He felt as though Emma was lost to him. Was he going to lose this girl too?

'You wouldn't remember me for a minute,' he said.

Patience emerged from the hair, blue eyes wet, looking nothing like a child but much more like a very desirable young woman, her skin was so pretty in the candlelight, he wondered what it was like to the touch.

She would have picked up the candle and gone, but he got hold of her. Somehow in his mind she and Emma got mixed up and turned around, because he thought of all those times when he wished he had held Emma in his arms, when he wished he had not left her. Was he going to do the same again? She was so beautiful in the candlelight, more beautiful than he could remember, creamy skin and pink lips.

He tried to stop himself from kissing her, but he didn't succeed. How stupid that he should succeed when he loved this girl so much less than he had loved Emma. Perhaps 'had' was the important word here. Emma had somebody else. He could have prevented it, he could have stayed with her, he could have done what he was doing now, hold her soft body against him, kiss her mouth. Why he had not done so, he couldn't understand himself. Emma was lost to him now, but this girl was not, and he needed her, he needed the comfort, the closeness.

She didn't stop him from kissing her. Somehow he wanted to avoid the responsibility, but he thought she should, and then he thought he should, but although he kept on telling himself he should let her go, he couldn't. It was like being two people, one watching and judging, and the other putting her down on the rug before the fire and kissing her neck and her throat and—

He stopped abruptly, not looking at her, not looking at anything really, only aware that this was not the right thing to do, reminding himself of who he was, and to his surprise it was himself and Emma that he hated, for somehow getting everything wrong. Patience didn't move. He had thought she would. He had thought any respectable girl would have got up and run away, but she didn't, she lay there and looked up at him from starred eyes. Her shoulders were almost naked. He tried not to look at her, because he wanted her so much. He tried to tell her that he was sorry, but the words sounded so stupid in his head that he couldn't say them.

In the end, after the quietness of the night took over completely, she gave a little sob and got up and ran away. Josh could not believe what he had done. He couldn't excuse himself because he was worried about his father, that wouldn't do at all. He called himself stupid and worse. He wished he could apologize to her, but he knew that wouldn't be enough or welcome.

Over the next few days, Patience avoided him. In the end he waited until she was alone in her bedroom one evening and knocked on the door. There was no response. He went inside, only to find she turned around, staring, and said, 'You shouldn't be in here.'

'I need to talk to you.'

'You can't.'

'Patience, please. There's nowhere private but here. May I come in?'

Josh shut the door.

'I don't know what to say now,' he admitted.

She sighed and looked straight at him and she said, 'It was my own fault. I encouraged you. I wanted you to fall in love with me so that I could reject you.'

'And now I have. Is that what you want? You want me to go away?'

She didn't say she did, and all he could think was how much he wanted to touch her. It was as though the boy who had been so sensible, so contained, so unworldly and dedicated, died right there and then, and all he wanted was to pull her clothes off her and get as close as he could.

'You're compromising us both,' she said, pulling away.

'I want to marry you.'

'No, you don't. You just feel guilty, responsible. I don't need a poor boy with a conscience to marry me.'

She turned her back and walked away and Josh was angry. For several moments he stood there, trying not to be the stupid boy whose pride was hurt, reminding himself of who he was, and then he went after her and got hold of her and turned her to him. He kissed her until she was warm and sweet in his arms.

'You will marry me.'

'I will not.'

'Oh yes, you will.'

It was a valuable lesson, he thought, afterwards, to find that you were at the mercy of your nature, and all those fine words, all that striving to do the right thing, was undone in seconds because you were young and wanted a girl as much as this. If she had not managed to put up a fist against him, he was never quite sure later whether he would have stopped himself from putting her down on to the bed and having her. There were a great many times when he wished he had.

'I'm going to go to your father and ask him,' he said, as Patience put some space between them.

'He will never allow it.'

'You do want me to?'

'Yes. No. I don't know.'

'I'm going home soon. I won't be coming back.'

She looked at him and all the longing and love was in her face. Josh went off in search of Diarmud Matthews.

'Mr Matthews, may I speak to you?'

Diarmud had just come in from a business dinner and taken off his wet things, and was about to join his wife by the fire, but he said, 'Yes, certainly,' and ushered Josh into the nearest room, the small sitting room. It was empty, a pretty room which overlooked the garden but just now was shuttered against the night, thick red winter curtains drawn over the windows and a fire high in the grate.

'You haven't had bad news, I hope?'

'No, no, nothing like that. I don't know how to say it.'

Diarmud smiled.

'There speaks the preacher.'

'It's different when it's . . . to do with one's self. I hope you're not going to think I've taken advantage of your hospitality or abused your trust. I'm never going to have anything much to offer, I . . . Would you give me your permission to ask Patience to marry me?'

Diarmud looked down and then he sighed.

'Oh dear,' he said. 'I had a feeling this was going to happen. What a charming romantic idea for my daughter to marry a penniless preacher.' Josh was surprised to find that a man he thought had liked him had only liked him when he thought there was no threat. 'Her mother would never forgive me if I let it happen. We did wish we hadn't asked you here the moment you arrived. I'm sorry, but I don't think I can let you address my daughter. I have nothing against you, indeed I'm very fond of you, but I want her to look in higher places. We won't discuss it again and I shall trust you to say nothing to her.

'I have been busy on your behalf. Perhaps just as well in the circumstances. As soon as you are finished with your studies here, you are to go home to take over from your father, hopefully as a temporary measure. I'm sure he will recover soon, and you will be able to take up a ministry of your own.'

'Thank you for that.'

'Not at all. Now, I think you have studying to do. I, however, will join my family around the fire.'

Josh hadn't been sat down at the little table in his room for very long when there was a soft knocking and Patience came in.

'What did he say?'

'He said no.'

'You must have known he would.'

'He called me "a penniless preacher".'

'You are,' she pointed out.

'I know, but it hurts to have somebody say it. He told me I wasn't to discuss it with you.'

A knocking on the door made her turn around, and when the door opened, her father stood, his demeanour somewhere between accusing and apologetic. She looked at him for several moments and then she said, 'You told him he wasn't good enough for me, didn't you?'

'Yes, I did.'

There was silence. She turned back to Josh, smiling a little.

'Because he doesn't have any money?'

'Patience . . .'

'He has perseverance, education, and he's brilliant, you told me so yourself.'

'I didn't realize things had gone as far as this.'

'He's very young yet. He could do well.'

'He's going home when he's finished here. His father is ill. He will have to keep his family, parents and two younger brothers. Josh couldn't afford to keep you in gloves. You're used to a different kind of life. You would hate it.'

'I didn't think I was such a shallow creature,' Patience said.

'People have different ways of living. You're not cut out to be a poor minister's wife. The only way you could possibly be married would be if you both stayed here, and that's not going to happen.

'I'll marry him and go with him.'

'You will do nothing of the kind.'

Patience looked defiantly at him and ran from the room

'You had no right to address my daughter without my permission. No man of integrity would have done so,' Diarmud said, and he followed her.

Patience went to her mother, who had long since been told of her feelings for Josh.

'I didn't know that you hadn't told my father.'

'I have tried to mention it several times, but I had the feeling he was very much against it and I didn't like to tell you when you were happy and doing such a lot of good work. You want me to speak to him?'

'Yes, please.'

Patience hovered in the hall the next evening, while her father and mother talked in the study, and since the door was not quite shut, she could hear most of the conversation.

'She'll forget him in time,' her father said.

'The way I was supposed to forget about you, do you mean?' her mother said. Patience was surprised that her mother spoke more sharply when they were private together.

'What?'

'My parents were horrified when I wanted to marry you. Your mother was the daughter of Irish labourers, after all.'

'My father was rich.'

'Not necessarily much of a recommendation,' her mother said.

'And what does that mean?'

Oh my goodness, Patience thought, they're going to quarrel over me. How awful. How amazing.

'He stepped on a lot of people to get where he was. You know that very well.'

'I don't step on people,' Diarmud objected.

'No? You're stepping on Josh because he has a poor background. As though that ever stopped a man achieving anything. He could have gone sneaking behind your back, making up to your daughter, but he came to you honestly and asked if he could approach her.'

Not quite, Patience thought. He isn't as good as they think he is.

'He's really what you want for her?' Patience heard the disappointed note in his voice.

'No, of course he isn't.' That was a surprise. 'But she's turned down half a dozen well-bred men, all of them with money, one with amazing prospects. She's chosen an intelligent, hard-working young man. He's twenty-one, Diarmud, give him the benefit of the doubt. He may be going back north to help his family, but my guess is he won't stay there. You've heard him preach. He's wonderful. He needs the right wife, just like you did, you and your poverty-stricken, potato-growing Irish ancestors.'

Patience wanted to applaud. Her mother was very good at this.

'I think you're wrong,' her father said, more mildly than he was probably feeling. 'I think he'll go back there and the poverty and the people will destroy that tremendous ability. We need him here with us.'

'Then we will have to learn to let go of Patience. She feels this is right for her. If she doesn't marry Josh, she may never marry from sheer dismay and disappointment. We have to trust her.'

Josh came down the hall. Patience put a finger to her lips and they moved away.

'Eavesdropping?' he said.

'My mother is trying to persuade my father into letting us marry.'

'Do you think she'll succeed?'

'I don't know yet.' Patience stopped there as her conscience reminded her of what she had done with Emma Meikle's letters. If she told him now, she thought she would surely lose him, but if she did not tell him, it would be such a dishonest way to gain him. She could not bring herself to say it. She could not bear to think what life would be like without him.

A short time later, her father came into the sitting room, where she and Josh had contented themselves, waiting.

'I have to say that this is against my better judgement, since you're the only child I have, but I'm going to allow the marriage.'

He got no further. Patience, almost in tears, got up and hugged and thanked him. Josh was quiet. It would be all right, she assured herself.

Josh wrote to his parents. The reply from his mother was effusive, and he thought that they could not help but be pleased at the connection. He was surprised that his mother cared for such things. It occurred to him that perhaps she had suspected his regard for Emma and was relieved, or was it just that she knew a minister must have a good wife? She said they were so glad he and Patience would be coming home, and only sorry that the journey was so far, and that his father would not be well enough to attend the wedding.

He and Patience were to be married when his studies were finished early that summer. Her mother was making the arrangements. Patience had said to him that if he preferred to wait, they could be married later in Durham, but that would mean them being parted for however many months they were delayed. He didn't see the sense to that and told her so.

He must go north, so she would go with him as his wife. He knew she would prefer to be married here with family and friends around her. His only concern was that she grew quieter as the weeks went past. At first he didn't notice, he had so much to do, but as the wedding date drew nearer and he saw how pale and thin she had become, he took her aside one evening and in the privacy of the study said to her, 'If you have changed your mind, I will understand.'

Patience looked at him from panicked eyes.

'I haven't changed my mind.'

'Brides are meant to be happy.'

'I am happy.'

'You don't look it. I don't want you to regret this. Please, just tell me if you've decided I'm too poor or too dull or both.'

'You're neither,' Patience said, not crying, 'and I do love you very much. It's just that . . .'

'It's just that what?' Josh said, taking a step towards her, so that she ran out of the room.

After that, every time he tried to talk to her she had something important that she must do. Her mother seemed not to notice, and when Josh suggested to her father that there was something wrong, Diarmud laughed and said weren't all brides nervy?

Right up to the day they were married, Patience intended telling Josh that she had destroyed Emma's letters. Every day she got up and told herself that this would be the day when she would be brave enough to do it. All through the morning, she would promise herself that when he came home she would talk to him, but always something got in the way.

There were so many arrangements to be made. She had tried to get her parents to agree that it would be a very small wedding, since Josh's family would not be there. Her mother said she had only one daughter, she had no intention of not making the very best of it, and her father said, if her mother wanted a big wedding, they would have a big wedding.

At first it seemed that she would be able to tell him, but

as time went on and the dress was made, the flowers were ordered, the invitations went out, the church was booked, so her decision to talk to Josh began to worry her and she began to feel cowardly about it. When he questioned her, and indeed when her mother did, she said there was nothing wrong.

The trouble was that the deception got bigger and bigger in her mind until she felt sick, couldn't eat, saw the wedding as something she wanted to run from, but she could neither run nor tell him. How ashamed her parents would be of her, and how humiliated if he should decide he did not want to marry her because of what she had done.

She decided she would not tell him at all. She would keep it to herself and gradually the guilt would diminish. She could learn to live with it, as she would learn to live with him. She felt better having made the decision, and to her surprise the wedding day was perfect.

The sun shone down, the service was pretty and she was sure that she had not made a mistake. She felt as though she would love this man until she died. She had been right, and he looked happy, at least, he said he wished his family had been there, and she knew that he was worried about his father, but he was pleased to be marrying her. She could not help a fleeting triumph over Emma Meikle.

They would be travelling north the following day. She sensed on him an impatience to be gone and was eager to start her new life. Her mother and father would miss her. They had enjoyed the wedding. After it, they both pleaded tiredness, but she sensed it was also a reluctance to admit the married state which would take her from them.

Her mother had moved Josh into the room next to hers for the one night they would be there. It had a door between the two rooms, so that they would have complete privacy.

The trouble was that when the guests had left and the wedding was over, Patience found that she was unable to bear the guilt and could not look at him, even less let him touch her. Josh sat down on the edge of her bed.

'I wish you would tell me what's the matter,' he said.

'There's nothing the matter. What could possibly be?'

'A fine marriage this will be if we aren't going to go near one another for the next forty years.'

'What?'

'Every time I come near you, you run away.'

'Do you wish you had married the girl you left behind in Durham?'

He looked at her in surprise, as well he might, she thought, cursing her own tongue.

'She's . . . going to marry somebody else, I think.'

'Really?' This had not occurred to Patience and to her dismay she was quite upset about it. She had imagined Emma Meikle pining. She had taken Josh away and Emma Meikle had found somebody else, just as though it didn't matter.

'He's rich, important,' Josh said. 'Owns six pits and an ironworks.'

'Well, she can't have cared much about you.'

'Says the girl I chose to marry instead. I think I should go and sleep next door. You obviously don't want me in here.'

Patience managed to let him get up, but before he reached the door, somebody, and it could not possibly have been her, because she was determinedly not speaking, said, 'I burned the letters she sent you.'

Josh stopped, looked at her as though there was a thick fog between them, and after he had stared blindly at her for a short forever, he said, 'What?'

Patience was shaking.

'I put them on the fire.'

He went on staring at her and then, instead of losing his temper, like her father would have done, he seemed ready to accept this possibility.

'And were there many?' he said.

'Oh yes. She wrote often. I was surprised she could afford to do it. She didn't seem to have any money.'

'You read them then?'

Patience was beginning to feel like somebody who had decided to cross a shallow stream and found when she got into the middle that the water was up to her neck.

'Only to begin with. They were so . . . so badly spelled, so . . . badly worded.'

The silence which followed this became so large that Patience feared the room would not contain it. She wanted to tell him that she had done it for love, she wanted to tell him she had not meant to do it, but it was such a tawdry little tale that she could not utter any more of it, only stand there wishing she was anywhere else, anybody else.

'I see,' he said, and then went into the other room and quietly closed the door.

Patience wanted to run to her mother but she couldn't. She was married now. She didn't even cry. She stood there for a long time and then she undressed and got into bed. Somehow she felt that she did not deserve tears. In the end she couldn't stand it any longer. She went to him.

He hadn't even undressed. The night was fine and he was standing at the open window. It would only be dark for a few hours. There was no light in the room. He didn't turn around, though he must have heard her.

'I'm so very sorry,' she said. 'I didn't intend to do it. I was jealous. I wanted you. It didn't seem to be very wrong. You could never have married a publican's daughter. And you said yourself she's going to marry someone else. She undoubtedly needs to marry well.'

He didn't say anything, and for so long that she thought he wasn't going to, and then he asked, 'What did the letters say?'

'I . . . I only read the first two.'

He turned around then.

'You burned them without reading them?'

'Yes.'

'So, what did the first two say?'

'I can't remember. The second wanted you to go home and I knew you couldn't possibly do that.'

'They moved shortly after I got here, and since I didn't have the new address, she wouldn't have got my letters after that. And she thought I had given her up.' He turned back to the window. 'I thought she'd just grown tired of waiting for me.'

'I'm sure she did,' Patience said hastily. 'Look at what she's done.'

Josh gazed from the window.

'I think I would have accepted it in time. I never had anything to give her . . .'

'And now you will always love her. Is that it? Because you can't have her?'

'I don't know. People can't help what they feel, only what they do.'

'But you will forgive me?'

'Yes, of course. Why don't you go to bed?'

Patience went back into the other room and closed the door. She lay for hours. There was no sound from his room. Finally, when it was almost time to get up, she fell into a light sleep. She was still aware that she had to travel north today, to a new life. She would have given almost anything not to have to go.

Eighteen

The rain never stopped the day that Josh and Patience went north. It was almost as though it had been holding itself back the day before. They had set off very early, her mother and father going with them to the station, her mother complaining that she didn't see why they should rush away, they should stay in Bristol for a few days, and her father saying Josh's parents were eager to have him back after all this time, and to see the bride.

Patience was exhausted. She didn't want to be in Bristol. She certainly didn't want to be in Durham. She wanted to run away to somewhere nobody knew her, or the awful woman that she was, anywhere so that Josh would stop smiling and being polite and she could stop pretending that everything was all right.

At least, after her parents had stopped seeing what appeared to be almost everything she owned on to the train with her, they waved her out of sight and she was able to lie back, close her eyes and ignore her surroundings.

Food had been packed for them. She ate nothing. Josh read a book and didn't speak to her, and finally, after a long while, the steady rhythm of the train lulled her to sleep.

They had to change trains more than once and there were delays with the luggage and with the connections, and the rain made the day dark. It was very late by the time they reached the little town where Josh's family lived. His mother and brother were there to meet them. Wesley was a tall skinny youth with nothing to say, and Mrs Castle said only, 'The train is very late. We've been waiting here an age.'

She clicked her tongue over the amount of luggage and

Patience was obliged, for the first time in her life, to carry heavy suitcases through narrow dirty streets. She was weary from travel and emotion, and from Josh not talking to her, but even laden with bags she was astonished at how poor the little town was.

They walked across the road and up a steep hill and then into a narrow cobbled steeper hill, all the way up that and then a few doors along and finally they arrived. Her arms ached. She looked about her. Tiny terraced houses crouched there. They came past a pub, signs of merriment from inside, various men in groups walking past, workmen by the look of them, rather drunk, and she looked at the chapel, which was no more than part of the terrace, and the house on the end of it, which was to be her new home.

Inside was a very small passage which could not be referred to without a great degree of flattery as a hall, the straight steep staircase leading up from there. Josh's father came out of one of the rooms and greeted them, though nobody embraced anybody.

'I don't know where we're going to put half this stuff,' his wife said.

Josh and Wesley were employed for some time taking most of it upstairs, though his mother said there was very little space up there, but it would have to do for now. The youngest boy appeared briefly but said nothing.

Mrs Castle offered her tea, told her to follow into the kitchen. Patience had no knowledge of such places but was urged to sit at the square table beside the window while Mrs Castle made the tea.

'We don't stand on ceremony here,' she said.

She gave Patience the worst cake she had ever come across, and made her feel obliged to eat it. It was dry and tasteless. After she had forced this down, Mrs Castle said she would show her upstairs, she must be tired.

Patience dragged herself up there, and it was even worse than the rest of her day. There was a double bed, a big wardrobe and a chest of drawers. The room would not have contained anything more, it was so small.

'If you want to wash, there's some water in the jug, though it probably isn't very warm by now. You won't want to go across the yard to relieve yourself at this time of night. There's a chamber pot under the bed. I'll keep our Josh downstairs out of your road until you're ready for bed. We get up at five for prayers. I hope you sleep well,' Mrs Castle said, and went out, closing the door after her and leaving Patience by the almost non-existent light of a single candle.

Patience was horrified. She had no idea how to find any of her things in the multitude of suitcases which had been stacked one on top of another. The water was almost cold, the towel she dried herself on was small and thin. She had no night-dress. She did what was necessary as fast as she could, put enough of her clothes back on to cover her and then got into the most uncomfortable bed she had ever encountered, it was all lumps and the sheets were rough. The mattress must be very old, she concluded.

She could hear their thick northern accents from below, and wondered how she had got herself into this. She thought of the elegant house in Bristol, of her bedroom with the little writing desk, and of her parents, and the tears began to well up in her eyes.

She heard footsteps on the stairs and then the door opened softly and closed the same way, as though he thought or hoped she might be asleep. Patience lay like a stone, listening to him undressing and washing and getting into bed, and it was just so awful. She had not slept in a bed with anybody, and in such circumstances, in such poverty, she thought it was more than she could stand.

He didn't touch her. Even in the night, when he turned over in his sleep, he did it like somebody practised, as though he had spent all his time before then sleeping with his brothers and had learned to contain himself.

There was a lot of noise from the street. She was not used to it, and even when she did sleep, she kept waking up, thinking that the house was being invaded.

Just as it was beginning to get light, she heard a banging on the door.

91

'What's that?' she said, forgetting that they had nothing to say to one another, and she turned over, only to find the new minister with his head buried under the pillows.

'That's prayers,' he said.

Nineteen

Emma held on tightly to the idea that Josh would come home and they would be married. She repeated it to herself over and over again, and it would all be as it was meant to be, so long ago.

She dreamed about him more and more often. Sometimes in the dreams, he was just about to go away and they were standing under the thorn tree by the river and he was kissing her. Other times, he was writing to her to tell her that he would come back, or he was arriving and she was not there, or she was waiting and waiting and he did not come home.

One night early that summer, her father died, quite suddenly. Her mother awoke and found him and set up such a wail that both Lucy and Emma were out of their beds and into the room within seconds. This time there was no need, Emma could see, for her to run down the street for the doctor. She had never seen anyone dead before, it was just as though he was not there.

Her mother went into Bishop Auckland and sold her pearls to pay for the funeral. Emma had not known her mother had such a thing, a short string, perfectly matched.

'They were my mother's,' she said. 'The only thing I had left.'

Emma tried to protest but her mother insisted.

'We can't go on owing money everywhere. Let us at least try to deal honestly from now on.'

The following morning Emma was busy when Lucy fairly skidded into the bar.

'Josh is here,' she said.

Emma flung down the cloth she had been cleaning with

and ran into the back and there he was. She couldn't believe it. Her dreams had finally come true. Her instincts had been right. He looked wonderful, not as thin as he had been, and taller than she remembered, and he was wearing a lovely dark suit and—

She threw herself at him.

'Oh Josh, Josh, I knew you would come back,' she said.

'I'm so sorry about your father, Emma.'

He gathered her into his arms. Emma kissed him and after a second he returned the kiss and that too was even better than she remembered.

'You didn't write. I was so upset. I was so worried. You look, oh, you look even better than you ever did,' and she beamed into his face and touched his thick golden hair with her fingers. It was only then that he released her and stood back. He didn't smile and he didn't look at her after the first long searching of her face as though he was making sure she was real. 'I will give this up. I will. I never intended to do it, it was just that my father—'

'I know.'

'Do you? I knew it wouldn't matter to you, I knew that when you came back you would find some way of making everything right.'

'Emma—'

'I love you. I love you so much. I dreamed of you coming back, I knew it wouldn't be long now, and you are ordained?'

'Yes.'

'And you'll have a parish – you don't call it a parish, do you? I want to learn everything about it. I will become a Methodist and I will be the best wife any minister ever had.' She clasped him into her arms and it was then that she understood something was wrong, because he did not take her into his arms a second time, and when she hesitated he stood back and looked at her.

'Emma . . .' he said again, and this time she managed not to interrupt him. His face was empty of colour and his eyes were unhappy.

'Whatever it is,' she said, 'it doesn't matter.'

94

'I'm married.'

Emma had had some very difficult times in her life, leaving places because her father had run up debt so badly that they could not stay, lying in bed at night listening to her parents fighting, her father treating her mother badly, the day that Josh had left, the morning her father had been found dead, but this . . . this was on an entirely new level. It hurt so much that it didn't, as though his words had gone straight through like a knife and, however much she bled, there was no pain. That would come later.

She wished the time back just a few seconds, so that he had not said such a thing. Perhaps she had imagined him saying it and it was not true, or this was another nightmare of him not coming home, not belonging to her. How could he not belong to her? They were not two people, they had always been together since the moment they met.

'Married?'

'Yes. I wanted you to know before anybody told you. I've come back here with my wife because my father isn't well and I'm taking over as the minister until he gets better.'

She missed most of this. All she heard, echoing over and over in her head, were the words 'my wife'.

'I'm so sorry.'

Sorry? He was sorry, like this was something he could apologize for? Emma stared at him. She tried to gauge the expression on his face but he had carefully, deliberately, she thought, emptied it. He could not be doing this to her. He could not leave her in this desolate place she had reached in her mind, where she was so much alone. Night after night she served beer to the pitmen and sang the same songs, and during the day she helped in the house with cleaning and cooking and washing. Until now, all that held her together was the firm idea that Josh would come back and they would be married. He was her last hope.

He went on talking but she had stopped listening and eventually she turned and walked out of the room and into the hall, where Lucy had been listening. At least she didn't have to explain. Lucy was already crying.

'Oh Emma,' she said, 'and you waited for him,' as though Emma had had a dozen suitors.

'No, really, it doesn't matter,' she said, and she turned and walked blindly towards the bar.

She went back to the bar and cleaned as though there had been no interruption, and it was not long before Lucy came in and took her into her arms and held her and all around her the world fell apart while she cried.

'Oh Lucy, he never loved me, not really, or he couldn't have done it. He never loved me.'

That night, for the first time, Lucy ran the bar and Emma lay upstairs on her bed and did not sing. The world was a different place now, and hostile. It always had been there, it was just that she did not acknowledge it. Nobody talked to her about what had happened, they were all very careful of her, as though she had some illness. The following night she went back into the pub and sang, not for anybody, but because it was what she did, and it was not fair to expect Lucy to go on alone.

The vicarage lay beside the church in the main street, behind big gates and high stone walls. The gates were closed and it was quite intimidating, Emma thought, stepping off the pavement and opening the huge gate with difficulty. Inside was a Georgian vicarage with long small-paned windows, three stories and a lovely half-moon-shaped window above the door.

Emma knocked on the door and when it was answered asked if she might see the vicar. She was told to wait and was then ushered into the hall and then into a lovely big wide room lined with books, which looked out over a big neat lawn with steps down from a terrace and great trees in full foliage all around.

The vicar, whom she had seen at a distance, was a large, red-faced man. Emma introduced herself and was asked to sit down. There she told him that her father had died and they would like to give him a funeral. He had belonged to this church as a little boy, though they had not been back in the parish long.

'I haven't seen you at my church,' he said.

'My mother used to attend regularly when we lived in other places, but she hasn't had much time lately.'

'I'm sorry. Since you do not attend church, I'm afraid I cannot help you.'

'But we've always been Church of England,' Emma said.

The vicar would not be moved. Almost in tears, Emma watched the door shut behind her. She trudged up the drive. She went to the Presbyterian church and was frightened away by the severe Scottish voice which answered her knocking, though she didn't think the man was the minister at all. She couldn't understand what he said even when he opened the door.

At the Wesleyan Methodists they were short of their minister, who had had to go to Newcastle to attend his dying sister. There was no point in her going to the Catholic church.

She trudged homeward. As she did so she went past the Primitive Methodist chapel. It was mid-evening by then, and in the still summer night, the doors and windows of the chapel were open and she could hear joyful singing coming from inside.

After standing still for a few moments, she trod up the steps. The door to the vestry was open and there sat the young man she had loved so fruitlessly for so long. He was writing at the desk, paying no attention to the singing that was going on in the main part of the chapel. As he sensed her he looked up.

'Why, Emma,' he said and she burst into tears.

He drew her inside and shut the door.

'I shouldn't have come here.'

'Of course you should. Sit down.'

Emma gazed through the tears at the charming little room. The sun was sending all its last light through a window that seemed far too big at first for such a small room, and there was a little garden beyond it where old roses struggled red against the wall and a path was almost lost beneath yellow weeds. The room had in it an upright piano prettily inlaid with walnut, a desk, a huge black and gold clock, two shelves of books and a charming little fireplace with pink, green and white tiles, as though somebody had not been able to resist such levity.

'I thought to see your father.'

'He's not well. That's why I came home, to see to things until he gets better.'

'Then you wouldn't have come at all otherwise?'

'Probably not,' he said, without looking at her.

Emma sniffed.

'I went to the vicar but he won't give us a funeral service because we don't go to his church, which I suppose is fair enough, and then I went to the Presbyterians and then the other chapel, but it was no good. I don't want him buried without a service. He was my father, even if it's just for my mother's sake, and I don't know what to do because this is a non-drinking place and we run a pub and—'

'I'll do it,' Josh said.

She looked at him.

'You will?'

'Certainly I will. I'm probably the only minister in the area who knew him.' Josh smiled.

'And you can tell everybody what a wonderful man he was, how good to his wife and family, how kind and considerate.'

'I shall say all the right things.'

The relief made Emma feel so much better. She got up.

'Thank you. I'll go home and tell my mother. She'll be so pleased.'

Twenty

Mrs Castle opened all of Patience's luggage that day and discarded the majority of it. She kept holding up lovely dresses and saying, 'You won't need this again. We can put it to better use.' And when Patience protested, Mrs Castle looked hard at her and said, 'You're a minister's wife, now, Patience. What example do you think it sets these people if you go parading around in things like this?' and she held up a low-cut cream silk ball gown, and Patience silently cursed the fact that she had not overseen her own packing. She had been too busy confessing such sins as she had to a man who didn't want her, she thought savagely.

'I'll need something for special occasions,' she said.

His mother didn't quite laugh, and Patience saw the lines on her face and how thin and tight her mouth was as she said, 'We don't have special occasions that call for cream silk. We don't have room for all these things and I can't imagine what made you think you would need any of it.'

'I didn't do the packing.'

'Weren't you a lucky lass, then, to have somebody else to do it.'

It occurred to Patience then for the first time that Josh's parents had had no real idea as to the kind of society he had aspired to in Bristol. They had just thought she was a well-brought-up chapel girl.

'Mrs Castle,' she said, 'this is all completely new to me. I don't know how to do any of it. I'll need your help.' And that was when Josh's mother sat down suddenly on the bed and said, 'Eh, lass, didn't you know what you were getting yourself into?'

'I love him,' Patience said, and immediately she knew it was the best thing you could say to the mother of the man you had married.

'I'll tell you what, while they're all out and Mr Castle's asleep, let's go down and have some tea and then we'll sort the fancy frocks you really feel you can't give up, and I'll stow them at the back of the big wardrobe in my bedroom so that when our Josh takes the world by storm you'll do him proud.'

They duly left the mess of luggage and dresses and went down the steep stairs, which even now Patience was getting used to, and drank tea over the kitchen fire, and Mrs Castle confided to Patience that they were so pleased he had decided to marry her, because they had suspected him of having feelings for a girl who came from a very bad family, her father had been a publican, a drunk and a gambler, and her mother had been one of those pathetic women who let her husband grind her underfoot.

'They run the most scandalous public house in the whole place, just down the road—'

'She's here?' Patience said, in alarm.

'The Ivy Tree Hotel. A den of iniquity. And she is the most brazen thing you've ever set eyes on. She gets up and sings in front of the pitmen like a music hall turn, and there's drunkenness and fighting outside the place nearly every night. It's a sin and a shame to see the way those pitmen spend their wages on drink when they've wives and children at home with hardly a crust on the table or a rag to their backs,' Mrs Castle said, and Patience began to feel better than she had felt in weeks. She had been right, Josh could never have married the apparently infamous Emma Meikle.

When they had finished their tea and gone back upstairs to the suitcases which held her most alluring nightdresses, instead of pursing up her lips and dismissing them, Mrs Castle said, 'I think you should hang on to these, don't you?' and folded them all up very neatly and put them into one of the long drawers of the dresser, and though she didn't say any more, Patience's face warmed and she turned away.

She wondered for how long Josh was going to behave like a stone. She had the feeling that all the diaphanous nighties in the world wouldn't make any difference.

Twenty-One

Emma was sitting alone in the bar on the morning of her father's funeral when she heard a noise at the door. When she unlocked it she found Daniel Swinburne standing outside. As she turned he followed her into the room.

'Is he really dead?' he said.

'Yes, he is. Pleased, are you? My mother is crying over a man who treated her badly for twenty years. Can you imagine?'

He didn't say anything.

'I don't think I'm going to go on singing for you,' she said, as though he had spoken. 'After all, you've achieved your object. You can put us out if you want, we can always move on.'

'It was never about the song,' he said.

'Wasn't it? You made a great fuss and performance for something it was not about.'

Daniel didn't say anything to that. Emma looked at him and something about his downcast face made her relent.

'It wasn't your fault,' she said. 'He drank until it killed him. I think he knew he wasn't going to live for much longer, that's why he came home. He wanted to be back here, and in a daft sort of way, I think he wanted to see you again.'

Daniel looked at the floor.

'He did, didn't he?' Emma said.

'I think so, yes.'

'Even though he knew you hated him?'

'Yes. I'm sorry he's dead,' Daniel said, and he stumbled out of the door.

*   *   *

Emma had not left the vestry long when Josh looked up and to his surprise his mother came in.

'What was that lass doing here?' she said. 'Does she not know any better than to bother you, and do you not know any better than to let her? You are married and people around here have nothing else to do but gossip.'

'Her father has died. She wanted me to take the service.'

'I hope you said no. They're nothing to do with us. He was a drunken, gambling wastrel and she had no right to come here and expect anything, especially after everything that's happened.'

'I told her that she can have the service on Thursday morning,' Josh said.

'Whatever made you say such a thing?'

'It could have something to do with my being the minister.'

'They're not Methodists. They're not even Christians as far as I can judge,' his mother said. 'Your father will be horrified.' And she stamped out.

Josh lingered there, not wanting to face more wrath from his parents, and even less inclined to go back while his wife might still be awake, but even when he went back to the house in the quiet, his father was sitting in an armchair and said as he reached the stairs, 'Is that you, Josh?'

Josh went reluctantly into the living room.

'Do you want a hand to bed?' he said.

'Come in here a minute.'

Heart going all the way to his feet, Josh closed the door.

'It was brave of you to take the service for Emma's father.'

'Was it?'

'It was the right thing to do. Your mother is naturally upset. She never liked Emma. She was always afraid that you would want to marry her and it would have been impossible.'

'She says people will talk.'

'Let them,' his father said. 'It was a good decision. Now you can help me to bed.'

*   *   *

There were not many people at the funeral, though Emma was grateful to see that Brendan had come for her sake. Daniel Swinburne came in at the last moment and sat at the back. Some of the off-duty pitmen came, those who used to drink with him, those who had liked his wit, and one or two who had known him as a boy and had known his family. Emma was grateful to them all, because a lot of them had never been in a chapel before, and some of them, especially the Anglicans and the Catholics, weren't supposed to, she thought. She was most grateful of all to Josh. She hadn't seen him in his official capacity before, and he was very good. He made everything easy. He sounded sincere when he talked about her father, and he managed to find good things to say about him which were not lies, and she could tell how pleased her mother was.

Within days the house was lighter without her father's presence. Her mother was almost happy, and Emma didn't blame her. Nobody shouted. She didn't have to share her bed. Nobody was drunk, and Emma and Lucy ran the bar competently between them. A lot of the miners said they were sorry about her dad, and nobody remarked that she no longer sang 'The Oak and the Ash and the Bonny Ivy Tree' or that Mr Swinburne did not come to the hotel any more, or at least they said nothing to her. What they said behind her back Emma didn't like to contemplate. She knew that several waspish women in the village had thought she had managed to attract the attentions of the biggest catch in the area, having no notion that he was taking a subtle form of revenge on her father for whatever secret there was between the two men.

Emma didn't like to say so to her mother, but during her father's illness over the past weeks, she was beginning to make some headway with what they owed, because he was not wasting what they were making, but it was a struggle. She was beginning to think they would be in debt forever.

Lucy had got a job at the doctor's house, cleaning, and Rosamund was working at the corner shop. They came back with stories, Rosamund scornful that anybody could think Mr Swinburne would be interested in their Emma, Lucy distressed, especially when so many of their customers had been in the bar that first night when her father had been so upset at her singing the song, and Daniel had been so awful, but she supposed people made up stories to suit themselves.

They would be relieved, no doubt, thinking that perhaps Daniel Swinburne would look at one of their daughters with favour, though, as far as she could gather, he did not. There were no stories about him after that. Most of her information came from Brendan and he said that Daniel had no girl, no friends, did nothing but work.

'He's always at the office,' Brendan said. 'It doesn't matter what time you come off shift, the lights are always on. I don't think he ever goes home. I suppose you don't when you've got nowt to go to. And he doesn't expect the men to do owt he can't do himself. He's a good lad, for all he's a Swinburne.'

Twenty-Two

The world that Josh had thought he was coming back to had gone just before he did, like all the best dreams. Instead of the lovely dales town, he had the awful little pit village and, instead of the woman he loved, some woman who—

He stopped himself there. It was not Patience's fault, at least, it was, but no more so than his own. She had burned Emma's letters. It was not exactly the world's biggest crime or gravest sin. And he must not call her names even in his mind. She did not deserve it. The fault was in him that he had been vain enough to think his fate was to go off to Bristol and leave Emma. He could not think what had possessed him; it was certainly not the voice of God, but his own wilful stupidity. Who had he thought he was?

It took him some time to recover from Emma's accusations, her tears, the awful way that she had been hurt, and in the meantime, his father was not well enough to attend to any of the duties he had taken on, so at least there was work to keep him occupied. The nights were different. He and Patience lay turned away from one another. What she did during the day he had no idea, because he didn't ask her and she didn't ask him and she didn't volunteer any information. Nobody seemed to understand that there was anything the matter.

It had been hard coming back in other ways too. His mother treated him as she had always done, and he was used to being treated with respect. To her he would always be her child and not the minister, and it was difficult to go from preaching in the chapel and at other chapels, having the people respect him for what he was trying to do, and his mother telling him that if he didn't eat what he was given he would get it for his next meal.

He couldn't eat. Wesley was forever taking food from his plate when her back was turned. That had been one good thing about coming home. Wes was now as tall as he was and had turned into somebody Josh thought he might like. Harry was still very much a boy, but it was Wesley who came to him during the second week they had been back and said to him, 'Is summat up?' His mother would have corrected him. She hated the local dialect, but then Wes was too bright to use it in front of her. How had he gauged so well that Josh needed to hear just that?

They were in the vestry, a little room just as you went into the chapel. The chapel did not feel like his, his father had been there, and his influence was everywhere; but his mother, in some unconscious wisdom, had moved all his father's things from the vestry into the little study at the house, so that it was completely empty and therefore was a place Josh could make his own.

Josh took to spending a lot of time in there to escape from Patience and from his situation, and the family, and even from the rest of the people, because few people would come in there without being asked, and interrupt what they assumed was important work, whereas mostly Josh sat and looked out of the window and wondered who was the complete and utter fool who had taken his place.

'Wes, come in.'

'So, what's up then?'

'Nothing.'

'Liar,' his brother said. Josh was taken aback. Nobody said things like that to him. He couldn't help but grin.

'You all right, Wes?'

'No, I'm bloody not,' Wes said, and Josh did another double-take before restraining himself from saying what the minister would have said.

He closed the door in case anybody should hear his brother swearing, and Wes sprawled his ungainly limbs across a chair and said, 'They want me to do what you did. They think I'm you. I have to study all the time and I'm no good at it. How can I tell my dad I'm not going to do what he wants me to do, when he's ill?' Wes squirmed around in his chair.

Josh sat down at the desk.

'What do you want to do?' he said.

Wes didn't look at him.

'Mr Swinburne has offered me clerk at the ironworks.'

'And you want that?'

'Aye, I want it,' Wes said, as though it should have been obvious. 'Only I daren't tell Ma. I tried to tell her and she brayed me.'

Josh couldn't help but smile at the picture this conjured in his mind. His brother was over six foot, his mother was about five foot two.

'You want me to tell her? What if she brays me?'

'And have the Almighty after her? Talk to them for me.'

'All right.'

Wes sat.

'So?' Josh said.

'So, aren't you going to tell me what's up?'

'I said—'

'The blonde siren keeps crying in the pantry, and if there's any noise coming out of your bedroom, I haven't heard it . . .'

'Wesley!'

'Well? I am right about this, aren't I? It's Emma Meikle.'

Josh said nothing. Somehow it made things worse to think somebody else knew.

'Lust, was it, that got you to Patience?' Wes said.

'No, it wasn't,' Josh said, finally becoming irritated and realizing the partial truth.

'I wouldn't blame you. Patience is the kind of woman everybody wishes they had.'

'And Emma's not?'

'The men talk about her, some of it's—'

'You told me she was getting married.'

'Likely he didn't choose to, or he had her without.'

'Wes, will you stop doing that?'

'I can't help it.' Wes smiled suddenly. 'I have the infinite curiosity of the celibate. I can't think how you got a diamond like Patience to marry you, you poor slob, but you're making her miserable. Emma Meikle is not for you, not in your profession.'

'I wish I'd chosen something else.'

Wes looked at him.

'Did you choose it?'

'I don't know. I could have stayed here—'

'You couldn't have married her even so, not if you wanted Mother or Father ever to speak to you again. Your family's the most important thing, surely.'

'It doesn't feel like that,' he said softly, and when the silence had lengthened, caught his brother looking at him.

'I'm glad you came back, whatever,' Wes said, and then he launched himself out of his chair and went back into the house.

Josh stayed where he was, thinking of how he had already preached several times in this chapel which he did not think of as his, or even as somewhere he knew. It was a light building with many windows and pillars, ornate all the way from the front to the back of the chapel, with marbled paint, which was pretty. The pulpit itself was built in two different kinds of wood, and was decorated as though there had been money to spend, which he could not imagine here. Perhaps somebody like Diarmud Matthews had been here in order to pay for some of it.

He felt like somebody else took over within him when he preached. He could not possibly have done it of his own accord. He closed up the chapel and went back slowly into the house.

Josh was trying not to avoid his father. He went upstairs in the early evening light and his father was sitting by the window and the last rays of sunshine were upon his face. Josh had a sudden realization of what it was like to fear death, to be so very close to it and to think of a world that went on without you, how left out you must feel, how incredibly sad to leave all those who loved you.

His father heard him and turned slightly, and Josh went around the winged chair which his mother had placed by the window so his father would not be too bored with being so very often upstairs – the steep stairs were becoming impossible for him – and he saw the pride in his father's eyes and he remembered why he had gone to Bristol.

'It's good to have you here,' his father said. 'It makes me feel so much better, knowing you're there to carry on the important work.'

'Do you wish we were still in Weardale?'

His father laughed.

'Every man who has ever lived wishes he was in Weardale,' he said, 'or some place like it.'

Josh sat down in the hard chair where he knew his mother spent many hours.

'I've been talking to Wesley,' he said.

'About what?'

'About his future.'

'He knows what his future is.' His father didn't say 'lucky Wesley', but Josh could hear it. His father's future was uncertain, even for a man who believed in God and the hereafter. They had not talked about heaven. Did his father really believe in it?

'And what is it?' Josh said.

'He's going to follow in your footsteps and go to Bristol.'

'No.'

'Yes, he is. I haven't kept him at his studies all this time for nothing. He could have gone to work years ago. He's nineteen. I won't have it, Josh, I won't have the disrespect. I've kept him years and years after dozens of boys went down the pits—'

'You wouldn't have wanted such a thing for him.'

'Of course I didn't.' His father was angry. Was it wise to anger him or would he have to go back and tell Wesley that he must go and be a minister? He had the feeling that Wesley had already made up his mind and was only doing them the courtesy of telling them what he would do.

'He doesn't have a calling.' Whatever that was. People talked about it as though a shining light came to you and said 'hey, Josh, this is for you'. He wished it had happened like that, things would be a lot easier if decisions were made for you. Perhaps his father had, and therefore would understand such language. 'He's got a job.'

If his father had been able to get up from the chair unaided, Josh was convinced that he would have done so at that point.

'He came and told you?'

'He doesn't want to disappoint you but—'

'He does disappoint me. He does. He isn't the son I hoped he would be. He isn't . . .'

'Oh, I don't think that's true,' Josh said softly. 'He's intelligent, kind, observant, well read and bonny.'

'There's no point in trying to do that, Josh, I've decided he will go to Bristol to be ordained and that's final.'

When he didn't say anything, his father said, 'It's what we do. We try and help people. My grandfather and my father and my brother and me, we were all ministers, and my sons will be too. There's such a lot of work to be done, you know there is. People need us, look to us. If not, then where are they to look? Life is almost impossible. What are they to do if there is no help?'

'Wes doesn't feel like that.'

'He just doesn't know it yet. He will.'

'He has been offered a job with Mr Swinburne at the ironworks, in the office. It's a good job. It's the only way he'll be happy, and what is the point in his being a minister when he has no heart for it, no calling? You wouldn't want that for him?'

'Those Swinburnes,' his father said dismissively. 'That boy, he had no background, his mother's family were tinkers. His father's family were idlers, drunks, his father could have achieved so much but he didn't. The place is falling to pieces. They expect the miners to live in hovels and work the long day and ask for nothing. What good is that? His father treated him like I wouldn't treat a dog.'

'Did he? How do you know?'

'It's common knowledge. To have a child, your only son, and to make him call you "sir", and never to see him but once or twice a week for an hour. What kind of man loves his child so little?'

111

Josh considered saying more, but he could see that his father was exhausted.

He went off down the stairs and wondered to himself whether the ministry had really been what he wanted. It had cost him the woman he loved. Perhaps he would never be able to divorce it from the feelings he had for his family and the knowledge that it was his father's greatest wish.

Josh thought if his father took nothing else with him into the hereafter, he would have the idea that his life's work was continuing and his wife and children loved him and he had done a great deal of good. It was so much more than most men achieved, so much more than they hoped for, or cared for. Life defeated almost everybody. Josh had the feeling that his father would be defeated in his last breaths. It was the only way out of life into death.

That evening he could not face the idea. He had managed it earlier but when he went to bed the thought that he had been gone two years and so had lost those years out of his father's life – it was too much to bear, as well as having lost Emma and feeling as though it was all his fault, he had each evening to face a woman he thought he did not love and did not want, and he could not manage a single syllable, even just to be nice. She said to him, 'How long are we going to go on like this?'

'What?' Josh was taken by surprise.

She stood there in the candlelight, her golden hair in a long plait and her blue eyes so serious, and the whatever it was she was wearing hid absolutely nothing of her body, and he could not help but stare, she was so perfect, and she said, 'We're married. I know I was very wrong and I have no excuse, but are we to go on like this forever?'

He couldn't talk to her. He couldn't have talked to her even had she been Emma. He couldn't say, *My father is dying.* She had no idea of such things. Both her parents looked as though they would live forever. Living forever. It was a wonderful idea, if you had money and education and optimism. Otherwise—

There was a sudden noise from downstairs, raised voices, and he thought perhaps somebody was trying to break in, he could hear his mother and Wes, but when he had left Patience standing in the middle of the bedroom floor and run downstairs, Wesley was standing in the kitchen, looking defiant, and his mother had one hand up to her mouth, as she did when she was trying not to cry.

'You told me you would talk to them,' Wesley accused him.

'I talked to Father. He wouldn't agree.'

'How can you treat your father like this when he's so ill?' Mrs Castle put in. 'He only wants the best for you.'

'It isn't what I want.'

'Never mind that. You should remember your duty. We didn't keep you all this time so that you could go and work in a wretched pit office.'

'It's the ironworks office. Mr Swinburne says I can start on Monday.'

'Mr Swinburne says . . .' his mother jeered, though somewhat wearily. 'He's nothing but a jumped-up Irish tinker.'

'Mother,' Josh protested.

'I'm not going to discuss this any more,' she said. 'What your father says still goes around here, and there'll be no foundry office for you, my boy.' And she left the kitchen.

'Can't you wait?' Josh asked his brother.

Wes looked at him.

'This is not the way,' Josh said.

'Mr Swinburne said Monday and that's when I'm starting,' Wes said, and he went off upstairs.

Josh knew that his mother was crying in the sitting room. She always did such things in private. When he went in she was standing in the darkness.

'He's not going to take any notice, is he?' she said.

'No.'

'Your father will be so disappointed. You're not happy.'

This surprised him. He didn't think she had seen.

'I was so relieved when you decided to marry such a well-brought-up girl, but she isn't making you happy. I have the feeling only shame is keeping her here, and she's such a lovely girl. I don't understand. I was so proud of you when you went away and now you're . . .'

She didn't say what he was, and since it was obviously going to be uncomplimentary, Josh could only be pleased. He hadn't realized his mother didn't like him any more. It hurt so much that, when she went off to bed, he couldn't move, and stood there, smarting.

When he finally went to bed he was hoping Patience had gone to sleep. It was a vain hope.

'Well?' she said, as he closed the door.

'Wes is starting at the ironworks office on Monday. My parents aren't very pleased.'

She looked impatiently at him.

'I couldn't care less about your wretched brother,' she said.

'I'm just trying not to let my father get upset when he's so ill.'

Patience looked harder at him.

'You think you can solve everything.'

'I was just trying to help.'

'Help?' She got out of bed and covered the short distance between them. 'I don't know who you think you are,' she said as she walked around the end of the bed. 'You can't even help yourself . . .'

'Patience . . .' The walls were thin and he had the awful feeling that Wes was lying in bed with a smirk on his face, listening.

'You brought me here to this ghastly little place. I know it was my fault and I was good and sorry for it, but you set yourself up like some little tin-pot idol and you expect everybody to stand back and think how clever you are, how brilliant.'

'Patience . . .' he said again.

She threw the water jug at him, the whole thing. If he could have found his sense of humour it might have been funny. The jug was heavy and she was slight. The weight of water took the jug down. There was a huge crash – Josh expected his family at the door within seconds but nothing happened, clear evidence that everybody knew what was going on – and

114

then he was standing in a small lake of blue and white porcelain.

She started to cry and tried to get out of the room – where she was going at that time of night he had no idea – and he stopped her. She tried harder to get away and within seconds they were fighting. Josh had sworn to himself that he would never lose his temper again. She cried harder.

'You don't love me. You never loved me. You never loved anybody but your blessed barmaid. You miserable wretch.'

The trouble was, Josh thought, that she had never been as attractive to him before as she was now. He would have given a great deal to have kissed her and put his hands on her and – he stopped himself from such thoughts. What kind of man wanted his wife when they were fighting? When he let go of her she sat down on the bed.

'I will go back to Bristol . . .'

'You can't. Neither of us would stand the disgrace. Your parents would never forgive us. They didn't want this marriage in the first place. We'll just have to make the best of it.'

He got down and began picking up the pieces of china, and then he mopped the floor with a towel. Patience got into bed and turned her back and after that the house descended into quietness.

Upstairs, Mrs Castle undressed and got into bed without a word. Her husband was sleeping. She dreaded that she would wake up and find him dead. She did think though that since Josh had come home Christopher had begun to get better. Now the weight of the responsibility of his job was gone and, although he was still tired and staying upstairs a good deal, there was a lightness in his face which she had not seen in a long time.

Nobody else understood what they had tried to do. Josh had come back so full of himself he could hardly walk for pride, with a wife who had pretty white hands which never mixed a cake. Wesley was her favourite – she didn't like that but he was – and was her most engaging son so she expected more of him and gained less somehow.

And Harry, who would always be the baby. He was eating her out of house and home and still came to her with his troubles. He was the only one left somehow.

Twenty-Three

The house was cold. It was not the kind of cold you got used to, it was always colder than you thought it would be. The coldness went echoing back into the past, and sometimes, Daniel thought, it went forward into the future. That was the most worrying part of all. Sometimes he thought he could see what he would become, the vast echoing of the hall went on and on and it frightened him. He would become his mother, sitting over the kitchen fire, unwanted, wearing clothes which were dark and dirty, working each day for long hours to try to keep together the building which no one was putting any money into. Only her industry had held it together.

All those years when they had sat in the kitchen together and he had not understood, and he had thought they were nothing but servants and had no rights, he could not bear to think of it. But when he had understood more, he still had no rights. His father did not want to see him. And perhaps he was also turning into his father, who had sat upstairs alone or gone to the pits and the works alone until Theresa MacGrath died. Daniel could remember the first time he went down the pit, the endless darkness.

He spent more time upstairs after that, learning to read and write and figure. He had grown up never knowing what a normal family was like, though his experience had since shown him that there was no such thing as a normal family.

That did not stop him from thinking so very much about Emma Meikle, from imagining that they would be married. He had not seen a marriage that worked, he longed for such a thing. His mother had always been the servant, his father always the employer. They had not slept together, there had been no joy over their child.

He had gone to Emma at the Ivy Tree and listened to her singing every night and come back here and made up stories in his head about what it would be like when she loved him. The idea was so pretty, the unattainable was always so much better.

The house was cold. It was dropping to pieces. He always meant to do something with it, to get men in to restore it, it must have been beautiful once, but what was the point of a beautiful building with no one to admire it, and he had no money.

It was the house where his parents had not been married, where they had not laughed together or spent time, where his mother had been neglected and his father had been solitary and he had been . . . what had he been? The cold house echoed, vast above him, as he stood in the hall.

He moved forward from there into the kitchen where his mother had spent her days. Mrs Peters, who cleaned, had left the fire alight in there, banked down, it was true. Everything was as it should be. He thought he could see his mother's skinny form as she sat there, the pinny she wore, crossed over and tied at the back of her waist, and her pinched face and her thin hair and the lack of hope. Had she not learned to wish for anything? And had Allan Swinburne never loved her? It was a terrible thought, that they had lain together without love. Yet he had done that. He had gone to high-class whores in Newcastle when he could defy his body no more. Some of them were young and it was indefensible. Perhaps men were such creatures that they followed their instincts in spite of their intelligence. What a sacrifice that was.

He thought of parties and of Emma in pretty dresses, and he thought most of all how he would turn in bed and find the warmth of her there. He turned so very often to nothing but space and silence and the night hours. He had learned to try to dominate them. The morning would come after all, but when you had a difficult dream, and it happened so very often, somehow, to find yourself alone when you awoke was not so bad when the sparrows were up and twittering in the garden and you could hear the sound of pigeons' wings in the early light, but when it was so dark that you could not distinguish the shadows, the loneliness was like a tomb. It was how he imagined life to be when you were dead. Life? Was it life? And was he never to have anybody who loved him this side of the grave? His mother had not loved and his father had not loved, and it seemed to him that the whole world did not love, at least not in any kind of sequence – and Emma Meikle did not love him and the house was cold.

Twenty-Four

The summer was soon over, the autumn did nothing but rain and Josh remembered with affection the house in Bristol where he had been so comfortable. The grates of the upstairs rooms in his home were cold, bare, black and empty and the downstairs rooms smelled damp. The ground-floor rooms had stone floors with rugs before the fire, and they were treated to his mother's version of soup, lots of very hard vegetables in hot water, and bread which had to be dipped in the soup to be palatable.

Patience learned to cook and bake, she was soon better than his mother, but that was no great thing, and he seemed to be forever coming in at the door to find his wife down on her hands and knees scrubbing the floors. His mother was a great believer in cleanliness. Josh was only glad her parents could not see Patience's red hands and white face. He did not pretend to himself that she was happy. She could not have thought it would be like this.

The rain ran down the windows day after day and Josh trudged miles to preach at other chapels and spent many hours with various activities which would keep people occupied and away from the evils of drink and poverty, but every night in the little town there was drunkenness and violence and he and Patience would lie huddled in their bed and listen to the noise beyond the windows on the front street, the swearing, the fighting, the sodden laughter and the thick accents. He only hoped Patience didn't understand all of it, some was so vile.

It was Sunday. Even his mother told him that he had preached a very good sermon that morning, so he must have done well, but he was exhausted, he had been up most of the night with a dying woman. By the time they sat down to eat their Sunday dinner, all he wanted to do was sleep. That afternoon he had to be at the chapel all the time and in the evening there was another service.

'You've had a difficult day,' his wife said to him when they finally went to bed.

'You know what they say. The preacher only works one day a week.'

The house he had been to the night before was the home of the Wyness family, down a dark and evil-smelling passage which led to a backstreet. Josh had not been able to reflect that the smell might have been worse on a warm night, but the continuing rain made him afraid of the dark streets even though his reason told him that most people would stay indoors on such a night unless they had a particular reason for doing otherwise. He had been shocked at the state of the houses owned by Daniel Swinburne, and determined to go and see him about them as soon as he had opportunity. Workers should not have to live in such hovels.

The drunks were off the streets. Sometimes he prayed for wet nights for the rest of his life, so that he would not have to hear the men fighting and singing. Many were godly creatures and were harmless, but some could not stay anywhere for long without quarrelling, hitting out and causing distress.

He understood why, they had so very little in their lives. Many an intelligent man was here for lack of opportunity, and once he had taken a wife and had a child, he was caught, if he had any decency about him at all. Desire had a great deal to answer for, he thought. Why could not nature have made things different? It seemed such an irresponsible way to go on.

The strange part about it was that he felt he could no longer tell the difference between lust and love, because he thought he had loved Emma and merely lusted over the girl he had married, but of late he had felt sorry for her when he saw the hard work she did, he had wanted to tell her all the difficult things in his life, and he felt affection for her, or perhaps it

121

was cupboard love, since she was turning into such a good cook and baker, but several times lately he had wanted to make her laugh and had been grateful to come home to her at the end of the day.

He reached the edge of the passage and came out into the little yard, which several houses shared. The rain was falling harder now. He banged on the nearest door and it was soon opened by a young man of about his own age. Alec Wyness.

'It was good of you to come, sir, and in such weather,' Alec said, opening the door wide.

Josh stepped thankfully inside. He did not know these people yet. He could not distinguish one from another, he had not been there long enough, so his father had informed him, Alec and his young wife had not been to chapel, because they did not care to leave Alec's grandmother alone for any length of time, and since they had a baby just a few months old, Alec did not like to leave his wife with the double burden. Josh liked him already.

Alec led him up the steep and narrow stairs into the one bedroom. A fire burned there and the room was neat, clean, smelled only of sweet bedlinen and a few wild flowers in a tiny vase on the little round table by the window.

The old lady had been ill for several weeks now, and illness and age had their own smells, but there was nothing unpleasant here. The old lady, white-haired and pitifully thin-cheeked, smiled at him.

'Hello, young man,' she said. 'My, you are handsome.'

Josh sat down on the stool by the bed and took her hand.

'Gran . . .' Alec said, embarrassed. 'This is the minister.'

'Indeed? Well, all I can say is they didn't make ministers like you when I was a girl.'

It made him laugh and be pleased that the old lady had such courage in what was undoubtedly her last illness.

'What is your name?'

'Joshua Castle.'

'Ah yes, of course. I heard of your grandfather. We lived over near Darlington when I was young. He was a fine godly man. He helped a lot of people.'

122

She was talking too much for her illness, but nobody said anything, even as she began to cough and could not stop. Joshua could not help being a little afraid. He had been there when people had died before, but he had never taken the responsibility.

He wished there had been a doctor to do that, but then he thought it was not his responsibility either. Only God handled such things, everybody else did what little they could, his training had taught him that. He did not like to ask if the doctor had been, whether Alec could afford such things, whether there was a doctor who looked after the pitmen and their families.

The old lady was exhausted by her coughing fit, and lay back on her pillows, the brightness in her eyes gone. Josh held her hand as she closed her eyes, and watched her fight for breath. She gained it.

Alec kept the fire going and later, while the old lady slept, Josh ventured downstairs. There was a bed in the sitting room, and here Alec and his wife and baby would sleep. They had one or two good pieces of furniture and a few ornaments which were doubtless family treasures, in a glass cabinet some china, he could not see the pattern on it because the corners of the room were dark.

Alec's wife, Elizabeth, made some tea. The baby slept, the rain poured down the windows. Elizabeth, a pretty dark-haired woman, told him how glad they were that he had come, and Josh thought, as he so often did, that he had not been mistaken in his calling, however much he chose to be light about it, in privacy, to his brother. If he had not been there, who would have helped them? His father was not well enough to stir beyond the house, and only went as far as the chapel on Sundays.

They did not leave the old lady alone for long. Josh was not even tired and, through the night, was there whenever she stirred. From time to time, as she slept, he went to the window. There was nothing to see beyond the backstreets and the rain.

It was a long night, but Mrs Wyness was still alive when daylight began to touch the window. Was it harder to die in

123

the dark, he wondered, or, having got to the day, was it worse to have the light snatched away from you? Even now, in his most private moments, he could not quite believe that you were moving towards the light and towards God when you died, but what else was there, what hope if not that?

The old lady died in the early morning, and he was holding her hand and praying for her, saying the most comforting words from the Bible that he could think of. When she died, the baby began to cry from downstairs, and in that instant he understood completely what compelled people forward.

Elizabeth hurried downstairs, wiping the tears away with her hands, and Josh thought that the little house was full of love and that was what would hold them together.

Alec Wyness and his wife and child came to the Sunday morning service without fail after his grandmother died. Alec had no other relatives, but rather to Josh's surprise, he had a good friend, a pitman he worked with, Brendan Kinnear, a man who drank heavily.

Elizabeth Wyness came to Josh after chapel one day, when he thought everybody had gone outside into the cold autumn day, the service having been over for some time. With the baby in her arms and the sunlight falling across the pews in the empty chapel, she looked so beautiful – like a Madonna – that he could not help but watch as she moved towards him. The baby was bright-eyed, chubby-cheeked, half asleep in her arms.

'I wanted to have a word with you, Mr Castle.' She glanced back to make sure they were alone. 'You don't mind?'

'Certainly not.'

They walked to the front of the chapel.

'It's about Brendan Kinnear. I don't like him. I don't know who else to talk to. He drinks so much. He didn't use to be as bad as he is now, and I'm afraid that he will lead Alec astray, and I . . .' She blushed a little. 'This is going to sound awful, but I don't like the way that he looks at me. I'm frightened of him. He came round the other night when Alec was at work, and I had a job to get rid of him. He didn't do anything but . . . I'm worried people might gossip. Alec is not the same since his grandma died. She was like a mother to him. His own mother died when he was little.' Elizabeth stopped there. 'I didn't mean to go on and on, Mr Castle, but you're the only person I felt I could come to. He respects you. Will you talk to him?'

Josh didn't like to say that he doubted he could do much. He also thought that Alec Wyness, like many other men, would not care to have his affairs discussed, or thank anybody for interfering, but she must be very worried to come to him like this, so he smiled and reassured her.

'I will do everything I can, Mrs Wyness.'

It took Josh some time to think what could be done. He couldn't tell Alec his friend was upsetting his wife. On the other hand, he couldn't let it go on. He caught Alec on his way from the backshift the following day and said to him, 'Do you think Brendan Kinnear might change his ways if you tried to influence him?'

Alec looked embarrassed.

'I've done my best, Mr Castle. You're going to tell me I shouldn't keep company with him, aren't you?'

'I wouldn't presume to do anything of the kind.'

'He's been like a brother to me.'

'Yes, I understand you spend a lot of time together.'

'We used to. Now I see him mostly at work. I don't go anywhere near when he's drinking, you know I wouldn't do that.'

'And what does Mrs Wyness think of it?'

'She doesn't like him.'

Josh looked him straight in the eyes.

'She isn't a good judge of character then?'

Alec smiled.

'You're doing this to me on purpose,' he said. 'I'm caught both ways, for she can't be a bad judge of character if she's wed to me. I will try to get him to come to chapel, and if I can't, then I will give up the friendship, I promise you.'

Twenty-Five

Brendan was surprised to see Alec, and rather taken aback because he had been about to go to the Ivy Tree Hotel. He had been concerned about Emma lately, for she was out of looks and out of voice, she was positively skinny and many a pitman had shaken his head that the plump arms, round breasts and sweet voice had all gone.

Mr Swinburne did not come to the pub any more, and the men were saying that he had had his way with the bonny barmaid and thereafter given her up, she was so downhearted.

Brendan privately didn't believe it, but when some of the lads were drunk, they egged one another on as to who might give her one next, though in fact none of them would have had the nerve to approach her. Brendan thought that if she didn't brighten her ideas up, the men would start to go to other places. Her sister, Lucy, helped in the pub, but she was sharp-tongued and not nearly as pretty, and when the men did speak to her it was with downcast eyes and few words. Lucy would say loudly, 'Speak up, Brendan Kinnear, I can't hear a word you're saying.'

She knew them all by name, which was very disconcerting.

Brendan was not happy at having Alec come to the house. Not that it was his house, but it was always in such a muddle. There were little bairns running about, half dressed, with grubby faces, bare bottoms and snotty noses. Shannon, the eldest daughter, was feeding her baby in the corner of the room. One of the lads, Connor, was drunk and snoring on the greasy settee, and Ma was singing in the kitchen.

There was, he allowed, a wonderful smell coming from

126

there, because she was making broth for tomorrow, no doubt with ham and pease pudding in it, and there was leek pudding and gravy for later, which was already made. Ma sang and drank her gin and cooked, and the more she drank the better her cooking was somehow, but he saw through Alec's eyes and compared it to Elizabeth's house and was ashamed.

'I promised Mr Castle I would talk to you,' Alec said, gazing as Shannon moved the baby from one enormous breast to the other. Shannon had bright yellow hair and was concentrating, and the baby put up tiny hands to help, perfect pink fingers. The children ran around the settee screaming with delight and Connor turned over in his drunken sleep, smiling.

'Oh aye,' Brendan said. 'What about?'

'I said . . .' Alec paused and looked down. 'It's not good for you, Brendan, it's not good for your immortal soul to go on like this. I'm worried about you. I don't want you to go to hell. Why won't you give up the drink and come to chapel with me and be saved? You would be one of us.'

Brendan moved him out into the passage as the children's shrieks grew wilder. Ma waved at them when they reached the kitchen and greeted Alec as warmly as though she had not just seen him a few minutes ago. The kitchen table was covered with chopped leeks and carrots and turnips and there was a little trail of pearl barley, glistening like jewels where it had escaped from her efforts to get it as far as the enormous pot on the fire.

She took great handfuls of vegetables and threw them into the pot with such vigour that the hot water bounced back up at her amidst the steam. Ma took no notice of that. Brendan could not help thinking that when he came back from the pub, she would have left a mountain of dinner for him between two plates. Leek pudding was even wonderful cold, all thick brown gravy and soft white suet and dark green leek.

Brendan and Alec stepped outside into the backyard. It was a windy October night. The stars were moving around and it seemed to Brendan that he could smell the heather from the fells out there.

'Do you want to die and go to hell?' Alec said.

'I shall probably feel at home.'

'Burning for eternity?'

Brendan looked at him.

'How's Elizabeth? How's the baby?'

Alec lowered his voice and his face.

'She wants . . . for us not to see you any more.'

Brendan looked at him.

'But we work together.'

'We could ask to be moved at the end of this fortnight.'

Brendan looked at the stars. Alec Wyness was the only real friend he had.

'Do you know what the gyppos say, Alec? That each star is one of their dead. Is that what you think, that there's only Methodists up there?'

Alec shifted about slightly before he said, 'I'll ask to be moved then, shall I?'

'You do that if you must,' Brendan said.

When Alec had gone, Brendan thought of that day not long since when he had not been able to bear his life any longer without sight of Elizabeth. He was off shift during the day, so he went round. Alec wasn't there. She didn't make him welcome. He wanted to hold the baby but she made an excuse. He wanted just to sit for a few minutes and make a memory of her exquisite face. She said, 'Alec's not here and I've got a lot to do.'

Brendan thought she would have, trying to keep a house as clean as that. He asked her how she did and whether her mother was getting on well in the shop, and she answered briefly, 'I never see her. She wanted nothing more to do with me after I married Alec.' And Brendan thought, why did people do that to each other, making impossible conditions?

She never invited him round any more. Now she never would, and he and Alec wouldn't even see each other at work. The daft part about it was that when Brendan got to the pub that evening he didn't want a drink, he didn't feel like it. Emma wasn't singing, she wasn't there, and when he enquired of her Lucy only said, 'What's it to you, Brendan Kinnear?'

'Is Miss Meikle poorly though?'

Lucy looked through him.

'Aye, she's sick of men,' she said.

When she wasn't looking, Brendan ventured into the back of the house and there Emma sat alone by the fire. When he said her name most respectfully she smiled and said, 'Why, Brendan, how are you?'

He pulled his cap off his head.

'I was bothered. Are you ailing, Miss Meikle?'

'No, no, I'm just . . . tired.'

She didn't look well. The glow was all gone off her.

'Sit down,' she offered.

'I don't want to disturb you.'

'You're not. My mother and Margaret have gone out to see somebody's new baby. Is it busy? Should I go through?'

'Your sister's managing grand.'

Brendan sat down. They didn't talk. He tried to imagine what it would be like when he and Alec were on different shifts, but he couldn't.

From this room you could hear the noise the men made, but it was shut out by the door. Maybe that was what made hell, you could hear everything you wanted but you couldn't reach any of it, closed out forever, remembering what the taste and feel and smell was like, a roast dinner beyond the window, a foaming pint of beer with somebody else's lips on it, and Elizabeth Wyness letting him out of the back door and not even brushing against him as she did so. He had walked very slowly up the back lane away from her, and if that wasn't hell then Brendan wondered what other treats God had in store for him.

Twenty-Six

Patience soon forgot what happiness was like. She caught sight of herself one day in the one mirror the Castles seemed to possess, in the sitting room, and was taken aback at the plain little face which looked at her. A desperate wave of homesickness hit her and suddenly she knew that she couldn't stand this life for much longer.

The family were beginning to take her for granted, and in a houseful of men, that was no advantage. Harry and Wes were very untidy. They dropped their clothes on the floor, they did not help with any household tasks. In fact, she thought, they treated her like a servant, asking her where things were all the time and expecting her to wait on them at table. Wes was out all day, now that he worked at the ironworks office, but Harry was at home, supposedly studying. He spent a lot of time with his father, and as far as she could gauge, a lot more staring from the window, doing very little.

Josh didn't seem to notice that there was anything wrong, but then he was very busy, had taken over all his father's duties, and as far as she could see was managing them well. Mrs Castle was too much in need of the help to see how burdened Patience was, even more so now that Mr Castle had started coming downstairs every day and sitting most of the time over the fire in the little study, reading or writing and needing everything fetching and carrying.

Josh worked hard too, and a lot of it he was inexperienced with. He was, she thought, not much more than a boy, yet the people came to him with all their problems. He was thinner than he had been in Bristol, his mother's dreadful cooking,

130

his father's illness and his onerous duties had seen to that, but their failed marriage was the main cause of it.

He walked miles in the pouring rain and cold wind because he had said he would preach in certain places, and he spent hours working out what he would say to them. He was never idle. They rarely had time to speak, and the only time they were alone, if you could call it alone, when she could hear his brothers in the other tiny bedroom next door, coughing and talking and moving about, was when they turned away from each other each night into the gloom. She had begun to think it would never get any better.

She hated the little house where you were never alone and where there was no comfort, nothing to divert anybody, no outings, no help.

One night when he came home late, she said to him, 'Can't we get a maid?' as he peeled off his wet clothes. She was standing ready to take them downstairs and put them over the clothes horse by the banked-down kitchen fire so that they would air in the warmth of the room.

'A maid?'

'Yes, you know,' Patience said, 'somebody who helps with the housework, the endless washing, the looking after three men, the cooking, the baking . . .'

'We can't afford it.'

'Even poor people can afford it, I feel sure.'

'We can't,' he said. 'I'm sorry. I know you aren't used to living like this and I know the work is hard—'

'We must.'

'Patience, we cannot. Don't you understand? We only have the little that Wes makes in the office and what the minister is due. My father gets nothing now that I get his money, and there are six of us.'

'I can count,' Patience said. 'This is the most miserable existence on earth.'

'I'm sorry.' He put out one hand and she picked up his outer layer of clothes and turned away, taking a candle in one hand and the clothes in the other. She disappeared into the shadowed stairs.

Once she got down there she wanted to cry. She could hear the sounds from outside, the drunken singing from the Ivy Tree. It was too cold to linger, even down there. When she got back upstairs Josh was in bed.

'Maybe we could go and visit my parents,' she said.

'I can't leave. I have too much to do, and besides we can't afford it.'

'I'm sure they would send us the money if we asked.'

'I'd rather not ask just at the moment if you don't mind. They were good enough to let us marry. It was what we wanted. It seems churlish to ask for more. Can't you make do for now and later—'

'It seems I have no choice,' Patience said, and she got into bed and lay with her face to the wall.

'Patience . . .' He reached out with one hand.

'Don't touch me,' she said, and tried to move further away as he drew back.

It was a long time before she fell asleep to the sounds of the street, somebody shouting, something breaking, but in the next road, she thought, not near.

Twenty-Seven

Daniel was sitting in the bank manager's office. It was not a place he liked. The bank manager was old and he was looking patiently across the desk and he said, 'We can't give you any more money.'

'I wasn't aware you were giving me anything. It's a nice idea though . . .'

'Mr Swinburne—'

'I know. I know. I have no more collateral. You told me last time. The price of coal is going down, the price of everything else unfortunately is going up. I started off with a disadvantage here, Mr Benson, up to my neck in debt.'

Mr Benson coughed.

'Your father tried hard—'

'Let's blame him. After all, he isn't here and I blame him for everything else that goes wrong in my life,' Daniel said, and, unable to sit for any longer, he got up and wandered across the office to the window. It was not an endearing view, the back road behind the bank, slush, dirty puddles where the surface had gone into holes, the yards of the houses opposite, houses he owned, houses which were falling down, unsanitary, damp. The men worked so hard, yet he did not pay them well or look after them. No wonder they drank and fought and grieved.

He was despondent. He had thought that if he worked hard and tried harder and gave every bit of his energy to the work, there would be a future, there would be a point to everything. How foolish that had been. He felt like running away, leaving it all.

He could not bring himself to believe that his father had

been incompetent. His father had had a great many faults but he had always worked hard to try to improve things. They had never lived lavishly, owned carriages, other houses, any of the things which were considered luxury. He and his mother had been his father's luxury in a sense, in a very small sense, he thought while he gazed out as the sleet began yet again.

'I don't know what to do, Mr Benson,' he said, and then wished he hadn't, but the trouble was he had nobody to talk to, nobody to consult. 'I can't even keep decent houses over my workers' heads.'

'I don't see what more you can do,' Mr Benson said softly. 'If you go any further you will lose everything.'

'Do you think somebody had a good time out of it?' Daniel envisaged wild parties, women who needed jewellery, men who needed . . . What did men need other than a lovely wife, a child, a little comfort? He would have settled for that. Perhaps the less you were prepared to settle for, the less God gave you, like some bargain which could never be settled, that God dared you to want so much more, stood back admiring those who took and turned his back on those who were prepared to compromise.

Mr Benson coughed as though he shouldn't say what he did.

'Lawyers are the only people who get anything out of things like this.' Mr Benson clicked his tongue over the idea of lawyers having a good time. It made Daniel smile, since his solicitor didn't look as though he had ever had a good time. He had never married, had no children, had no home even. He lived in a horrible backstreet hotel in Durham, and his business was a series of dark musty little rooms which smelled of mice and stale biscuits.

Maybe, he thought, I'll end up like that. Worse still, he realized who the man was who Emma had liked so very much. His source of information was Wesley Castle, whose elder brother had come home to be the minister. That in itself would have been suspect, but Wesley was sometimes very open and had told him all about Joshua Castle, what a good lad he was, how kind, how he had spoken to their parents on Wesley's behalf, not like a brother at all, more like a friend. Wesley had also confided, some time back, that his parents had not been at all pleased to discover that, when they moved, it was to within yards of the public house which the Meikles owned. They had worried that their eldest son was keen on the eldest daughter.

Joshua Castle had come home married. That should have been a cause for celebration, and Daniel was only pleased that he could be sorry for Emma, almost as sorry as he was for himself. Matters were made completely intolerable by Joshua Castle, who turned out to be clever and capable.

People talked about how he was looking after his parents and brothers, how he took over all the duties his father could no longer perform, how he would walk miles and deliver brilliant sermons, and his wife was beautiful. Daniel hated Joshua Castle with an intensity which surprised him.

He had seen the couple together at a distance, and Patience Castle was stunningly beautiful, blonde and slight, and Joshua Castle was tall and wore suits which a poor preacher should never have been able to afford.

Daniel heard the silence behind him and realized that Mr Benson was waiting for him to leave.

'I'll not waste any more of your time then,' he said and went out, not quite slamming the door behind him.

He didn't go back to the pit, where he had intended to go, nor to the ironworks office, where he should be after that. He went home. Mrs Peters was cleaning, down on her hands and knees, washing the hall floor. His conscience told him he should get help for her, but he didn't indulge it. He walked carefully over the wet floor and went into the study, where the fire burned.

Coal was the only decent thing he had left, he thought, rather inclined towards the decanter of whisky which stood on a side table, except that Mrs Peters would know if he started drinking during the day, and she would be concerned. She might even tell somebody in the village, and that wouldn't do, so he fought off the need and sat down at the desk and began looking through the paperwork.

Where it all came from he didn't understand, since he had offices to take care of it. This was stuff for the house, bills which he hadn't paid, estimates for repairs which he couldn't afford. He tried to immerse himself in that, and was suddenly too tired to care. He hadn't slept properly in weeks, what with Emma and money problems and . . .

He awoke to find Mrs Peters saying his name. He was face down on the desk, his arms and whole body cramped. He blinked and looked at her.

'I've got the preacher in the hall,' she said. 'He wants to see you.'

'What?'

'The preacher, Mr Castle.'

'Oh.' How strange, when he had been thinking about Joshua Castle, to find the man in his house. Whatever could he want? Should he deny him, say he wasn't at home – except that the minister must have gone to a lot of trouble to discover that he was at home.

Mrs Peters went off to tell him to come in, and Daniel noted the time. He had been asleep for two hours, more. He sat back in his chair and prepared to wait, but his good manners defeated him. His mother had instilled these into him at an early age and he couldn't not get up and be civil and smile and greet the minister.

Joshua Castle came in apologizing for the intrusion, awkward, uncertain. Daniel was surprised, he had thought the man would be haughty or at least stuffy. Mr Castle looked almost as tired as he felt himself, with dark shadows beneath his eyes.

'I'm sure you'll think I shouldn't have come,' he said.

Daniel said, 'Not at all,' and was about to offer him a drink when he remembered he couldn't, and therefore couldn't have one himself. 'Do sit down. Would you like some tea?'

'No, thank you. I think I had better stand.'

He had a clear almost ringing voice, deliberately modulated.

'I have come here on behalf of the pitmen. Actually I haven't told them I'm coming, so that isn't quite true. It's just

136

that so many of them are in distress of all different kinds, and I know that you would like to help them.'

How very neatly put, Daniel thought.

'I would love to, if you could suggest a way.'

'I could suggest a great many ways.'

Daniel was reminded of swordsmen squaring up to fight.

'I'll save your breath for you. If this is about money, you've come to the wrong place,' he said.

'I don't think so,' Joshua Castle said.

Daniel hesitated.

'I'm not going to play the villain to satisfy you,' he said. 'I don't have any money. If I did, I would pay the men better and house them better. I would do other things. I don't have it.'

He could see doubt in the other man's eyes.

'You're not making a profit?'

'Not enough to pay more than what I owe the bank, and the men's wages. I'm very badly in debt, I always have been, and I'm not clever enough to make the money to cover it.'

'What about this house, it must be worth a great deal.'

'I don't own the house, the bank owns it more or less. If you can find somebody to blame, please do. My father left everything to his three sisters and me, equal shares to his surviving family. I can't even blame them. They aren't married. They depended upon him for their support and needed the money badly. By the time I had bought them out and sorted the legalities of it all, I was so far in debt I shall probably never recover . . .'

Daniel didn't get any further. There was a knock on the door and Mrs Peters put her head round.

'Able Turner is here. There's been an accident at the Delight.'

Never had a pit been less aptly named, Josh thought. Daniel Swinburne had fairly run out of his shabby house and along the drive, and the short distance between his home and his pit, and Josh had gone after him, not sure whether there was anything he could do.

Time went by so slowly, the afternoon and evening crawled past with a great many people gathered at the pithead as the sleet came down relentlessly. Emma was there with her sister Lucy, and he saw Elizabeth Wyness, though without the baby, and Patience close by.

Men came up and were claimed by their families, relieved they were alive and well. Others came up after that, grave-faced; somebody had been hurt. Many of them Josh recognized from his congregation and generally in the streets, and he was glad to be there, glad to see that some of the faces lightened when they saw him. More and more of them went home, and Josh saw Brendan Kinnear being helped out of the cage, and how he blinked in the light. He came across to where Elizabeth Wyness stood, not far from Josh, a little apart.

'Alec's bad.' And then he came to Josh. 'Will you go down, Mr Castle, Mr Swinburne said, but only if you're aware of the danger, he said to tell you. The roof could go some more.' Brendan glanced across at Elizabeth. 'Only, they can't bring Alec out and he's asking for you.'

Josh was surprised but he did not think, he went down in the cage with two other men. It was a very strange experience and somehow he felt ashamed that he had not been down a pit before, first the drop into darkness, then the bottom of the shaft and the dim lighting and the way that, once you set off walking, there was not much room because the height of the roof went down dramatically and the space narrowed at either side. He felt cramped and wanted to run away. It was the first time he had understood that he did not like small spaces. A fine time to discover that, he thought, attempting to control the fear that threatened his insides with big, beating wings.

And then he forgot about it. There, amidst the dim lamps, was a wall of stone, a black avalanche, and there Daniel Swinburne and the local doctor, Thomas Pike, were crouched, and beside it all lay Alec Wyness. Daniel looked up and Josh thought he could discern relief in his eyes, even though the darkness shadowed all their faces, but when the doctor looked up he shook his head.

Josh got down and spoke to Alec. He didn't remember afterwards what he said, and he wasn't sure the young miner heard any of it, he was in such pain, but he acknowledged Josh's presence with a word. Josh lost any idea of time. He felt as though he had stepped through the doors of hell.

Alec died somewhere amidst Josh's soft voice, and the words began to fall into one another, became meaningless. He had never felt so helpless or so useless, and he found himself looking around for somebody to blame. The doctor got up but Daniel sat there like he would not move again, as though he was expecting Alec would come back to life, sure that it had been a mistake.

The other two men took the doctor back to the surface. Left alone with their employer, to his own surprise Josh said, 'It was an accident, Daniel,' breaking two rules, first by comforting a man he badly wanted to dislike, and secondly by using the Christian name of somebody he didn't know well, who was above his own social level. He had the feeling that Daniel would not forgive him for either.

Daniel found his voice. It shook.

'I have to go up there and tell Elizabeth Wyness that her husband has died down my bloody pit and it was my fault.'

'Would you like me to tell her?'

'No!' Daniel was shouting. 'I suppose you think your Methodist ways will help.'

'Daniel . . .'

'And stop calling me by my first name.' Daniel glared at him from very bright eyes. 'Who do you think you are, you arrogant little shit?'

Strangely, it was the 'little' that upset Josh most. In an area where men were small for mining, he was six feet tall, almost as tall as the man who was shouting at him. In the silence that followed, Daniel Swinburne gave a brief despairing sob and then got up.

When they reached the surface, the sleet had turned to snow, as though that might help, that a white covering would coat the grief. Elizabeth Wyness didn't cry. She didn't rant. She got down beside her husband's body when they brought him out of the pit.

Dr Pike watched as Daniel turned to go back down the pit. The fall had to be cleared completely. Gradually people began to move away. Patience was with Elizabeth. The doctor looked at Josh and shook his head for the second time and then he walked away.

Patience went back with Elizabeth to her house. Josh thought he might go over later but he didn't want to crowd her. There would be plenty of time for visiting. He went home. It was very late by then and his mother, softly for once because she had been told what was happening, tried to persuade him to eat and then to go to bed, but he couldn't do either.

He went into the vestry. It was bitterly cold in there, so he lit the fire and sat down and tried to write. Hadn't he learned anything today? The words wouldn't come, just the image of Alec dying. In the end, when it was almost morning, he went out.

He didn't intend going to Langley House, it was just that he could see lights winking on the snow and somehow his footsteps took him there. He hammered on the door. There was no reply but the door was not locked. He went inside. The lights were all from one room, it was the same room he had been in earlier. He opened the door.

Daniel Swinburne stood near the fire with a whisky glass in his hand, and he looked up at the sound of the door and then he smiled.

'You don't give up, do you? I told you I haven't got any money.'

'That's not going to help,' Josh said, nodding at the whisky.

'How could you possibly know?'

'It was just an accident.'

'Yes,' Daniel said. 'Nothing to do with the fact that the pit is neglected. Someone is always to blame, don't you find?'

'You can't control everything.'

'God has a nasty habit of reminding me.'

'It wasn't your fault.'

Daniel went over to a sideboard, where the decanter stood. He emptied the last of the golden liquid into his glass.

'Do you think that's what they're saying in the village? 'Good old Swinburne, it was nowt to do with him that Alec died'? No, they're blaming me, just like you did. For their houses and their work and their lives. They hate me. It's useful having somebody to hate. They say, "He's just like his father was, and he was an evil bastard".'

'Don't have any more,' Josh said, nodding at the whisky.

'I can't have any more, there isn't any,' Daniel said, emptying the glass. 'Why don't you take your smug face home? I can't bear the sight of it. You have no right here. I'm not a Methodist, I never will be, so there's no point in you coming here thinking I'm going to give up my evil ways because a good pitman is dead. That is what you came for?'

'I just thought you might want the company.'

'What, your company?' Daniel laughed. 'What would I want that for?'

'I didn't think you had any family, and it's hard being alone when things like that happen.'

'It's your bloody fault I'm alone,' Daniel said.

'I don't know what you mean.'

Daniel, Josh realized, was very drunk, his dark eyes wavered and they were lit with bitter amusement, but all he said was, 'Get out of my house.'

'Daniel—'

'There you go, you're doing it again.' His eyes were even brighter now. 'Just who the hell do you think you are?'

'I know who I am.' Josh held his gaze. 'This wasn't your fault. You're doing everything you can. Isn't that what you told me?'

'What do you care? He's dead and that's all that matters.' Daniel turned away, his voice breaking. 'He's left a wife and baby. I wish it had been me.'

'Oh, very practical,' Josh said. 'Who would run things if you didn't? Everybody would be out of work immediately and we would all starve. Nice.'

Daniel's shoulders began to shake.

'It wasn't your fault,' Josh said again. 'You provide work

for all these people and mining is a dangerous business. They know that.'

'Tell it to Elizabeth Wyness.'

'I don't need to. She's a strong woman. She'll survive. And she has her baby.'

'I'm going to go and see her tomorrow. I'll let her have the house and there'll be money and I will do everything I can.'

'I'm sorry I came here today and went on at you,' Josh said, and Daniel turned to him. 'I didn't understand.'

'What did you think I was doing here, having a good time?' Daniel said with a hint of a smile.

'Maybe. People always think it of the owner. I will do everything I can to help, and if you should want anything you can let me know.'

Josh didn't know what more to say. The night was giving way to a white cold dawn and he was tired and in despair.

'I'm going to bed now,' Daniel said. 'Let yourself out.' And he went.

After Josh had gone, Daniel let the tears fall freely, but they dried as soon as they fell, and as he made his way upstairs, all he could hear was the sound of comfort and Josh's voice saying, 'It wasn't your fault.'

How many times had he said it? Daniel couldn't remember.

Josh had not been in the house long when his father appeared.

'How do you feel?' Josh said.

His father smiled. It was a smile that could light up the house, Josh thought.

'It was a shame about young Wyness. He was a good man. You did very well.'

'Did Patience come home?'

'Yes, when it was very late, I think. She's still sleeping.'

Josh wished him good morning and went upstairs. He was right, she was lying there looking so beautiful in the pale light which reached into the room from beyond the curtains. He very much wanted to get into bed with her and be held to ward off the images of Alec dying but he couldn't. And then she heard him and opened her eyes.

'Where have you been?'

'To see Daniel Swinburne.'

'Why?' She sat up as he made his way round the bed.

'He was very upset. What about Elizabeth?'

'Her mother turned up.' Patience pulled a face. 'I don't think she was pleased to see her but it meant I had to come out, otherwise I would have stayed. Have you been up all night? You look ready to drop.'

'Alec shouldn't have died.'

'Have you had anything to eat?'

'I don't want anything.'

Suddenly he couldn't see for tears, put both hands up to his face to cover it completely, his mind filled with the image of Alec, lying dead down the Delight. 'Have you ever heard a pit called such a stupid name? Have you? Well, have you?'

She came to him but Josh turned away.

'Josh . . .'

'It's a stupid name. It's stupid, it's stupid.' And he sat down on the bed and the tears fell through his hands. 'I wish I'd never come back here. I can't do this. I can't do it.'

Patience got hold of him.

'Don't,' Josh said.

'It's all right,' she said.

'It isn't. Why does God let people die like that? Alec had everything to live for and now it's all gone.'

She had him in her arms now. When she didn't answer, he took his hands away from his face and got hold of her and then he buried his face in her hair.

'Please just hold me a moment.'

She held him nearer.

'How can Alec be dead?' Josh said. 'How can he be?'

She hushed him, held him, it was enough for a short while and then he wanted to kiss her. He couldn't believe that he hadn't kissed her in so long, had no idea how she would taste or feel, and so when he did, it was so amazingly good that he wanted to kiss her again and then again, and she helped, she kissed him back, she put her arms so far around his neck that there wasn't any room between them.

Then that wasn't enough. He put her down on to the bed and hauled the nightdress off her and stripped off his clothes. He was only just aware that light came around the edges of the curtains and that they had never done this in daylight, how strange. Why didn't people? Or perhaps they did and it was just natural modesty to religious people not to, or just that they knew one another so little and were shy. There was nothing shy about this, with the household sounds going on around them beyond the door. Was it better because he needed it to be, or was it better because it made him feel more alive in the face of death, or was it because it had been the longest most difficult night of his life? Or was it for some other pitiful reason than all these? Whatever, this beautiful naked girl was giving herself to him and all the reasons in the world didn't matter now.

Twenty-Eight

Patience and Elizabeth had been drinking tea in the quietness of the kitchen when her mother walked in. She didn't even knock. She stood there in the doorway for a few seconds, letting the snow blow in around her, and then she seemed to remember and closed the door.

'Is it true?' she said. 'Is Alec dead?'

No beating about the bush for her, Elizabeth thought. Alec had not passed away or passed on or been taken from them.

'Yes, he's dead,' she said.

'I thought they might have got it wrong.'

'He's upstairs in the back room if you want to make sure,' Elizabeth said.

They had not seen each other in two years. Her mother seemed a lot older than she should have done, Elizabeth thought. Perhaps that was what loneliness did for you. Was her mother glad that Alec had died? Perhaps she thought she would recapture the relationship they had had between them before. She knew what it was like to have a child.

Her mother had not seen the baby. She looked but did not say anything, and it occurred to Elizabeth that her mother might even think the child an encumbrance. Elizabeth could not think that Alec was dead, she kept waiting for him to come in for his evening meal. She heard his voice, she felt his presence, the little house was somehow full of him, but for her now there would be nothing but funerals, arrangements, the endless time passing, and she would be waiting in the doorway, not actually but in spirit, waiting there during the long hours of each morning and afternoon, evening and night, for him to come back to her.

145

'What happened?'

She turned to her mother's question. She might even have asked it more than once. Did her mother really not know about the accident? She must have done, otherwise what was she doing here?

'The roof fell in.'

It was a common enough problem.

'You must go to Mr Swinburne and demand recompense.'

Recompense? As though Daniel Swinburne had done this on purpose, as though he had not come to her honestly and told her that it was his fault, that he would help her, that Alec was dead.

'Mr Swinburne said he would do everything he could.'

'Huh. I can imagine. Don't people always say things like that?'

'He meant it, Mother.'

'If his pit had been safer this would never have happened.'

'Things do happen. That's the problem. If we knew we were going to live to ninety, how different it would all be.'

'Those Swinburnes,' her mother said. Elizabeth knew it was just for something to say, and that everybody always blamed their employers, and that possibly the roof should not have fallen in, but even in the safest of mines there were accidents, because it was a risky thing, there was always the chance that something would go wrong.

Everybody involved in it knew that. Besides, somehow she knew that she could not blame Daniel Swinburne more than he blamed himself, she could tell just by his eyes.

Her mother admired the baby. It was getting late. Her mother urged her to bed. Elizabeth thought she would never sleep again. They kept the fire going, drank tea, sat over it and finally her mother dozed. The baby cried. Elizabeth picked her up, comforted her. Her mother slept on.

She thought that the night would go on forever, that it would always be the day when Alec had died. He had said he would never leave her. You couldn't trust men, she thought in amusement. How short a time it had been since they had been together. She ought to have known that something perfect could not last. He was dead, it was over. The dream was gone.

146

She looked at her mother in sleep and wondered whether that was what she would become, not dreaming of being more than one, not venturing out again for fear of being hurt, not thinking life had anything good to give. Was that really what Alec's death would have in its wake? The best was over?

Was he really dead? Surely he would have got back to her somehow, told her, let her know. They had been so close. It could not be that she would not see him again, not hear his voice, not lie with him in bliss in the upstairs room. Was this what life offered?

The baby cried again and her mother woke and offered to take the child, but Elizabeth would not let her.

'You can't stay here now,' her mother said. 'You and the baby must come and live with me. Mr Swinburne won't let you keep the house in any case. Miners' wives are allowed nothing once they are gone.'

Elizabeth could have shuddered over what living with her mother was like. There was something sterile about it, untouched, never moving forward, almost dormant. She did not think she could go back to that. She would go to the pit office and talk to Daniel Swinburne in the morning.

'It's not much of a house anyhow,' her mother said, looking around disparagingly. 'You wouldn't want to go on living here. Our house is much nicer than this, much bigger. The baby could have her own room.'

Elizabeth thought she would not want to be parted from her baby if she lived to be a hundred, and then she understood how her mother felt. Her mother had not wanted to be parted from her child either, had been jealous, unloved, neglected. That was what children did to mothers, Elizabeth thought. In time her child would do that to her, want to be without her, live without her, marry and have her own child and so on. Was it never-ending?

She was exhausted. When the baby cried again and her mother picked it up, she had not the energy to object. She lay down there on the settee and finally closed her eyes. Alec was dead and nothing mattered any more.

Twenty-Nine

Josh couldn't eat. He couldn't sleep, he couldn't write his sermon. He didn't want to be in the same room either with his family or with Patience. He didn't understand how you could be so close to a person, like he had with Patience earlier that day, and yet so lonely. She did not love him. He had not understood at first but he did now. She loved the strange status of his profession, the person who got up on Sunday in front of hundreds of people and told them what he thought, and they respected him for it. Sometimes, though he would not have said so to anyone, it was the closest thing to being a dancing bear. Patience had married the minister, she had gone to bed with the preacher and woken up with the boy, and she didn't like him.

They had made love and slept and when he awoke in the middle of the afternoon she was not there. He was so disappointed but there was nothing to do but wash and dress and go downstairs and carry on as though nothing was any different.

The night after Alec's death, when they had gone to bed, he had tried to get hold of her and she had refused.

'Did I hurt you?' he said, into the darkness.

'You don't care about me. What we did last night has nothing to do with love, you were upset and it had nothing to do with me. You would have been the same even if you'd been with a whore. It didn't matter who I was. In fact, I think you had no idea who I was, I was just a body, that's all.'

The real problem, Josh thought, was that he was too inexperienced to take Alec Wyness's death as part of his job, and she was right, he had been desperate for comfort, not eager

148

for his wife, but was there a difference? Was it not part of a wife's job to comfort her husband like that, in the most basic way, when the world was falling in around him. He wanted to tell her that there was more to it than that, but somehow he couldn't, or she did not give him the chance. She banged out of the bedroom and left him there. He ought to have followed her downstairs in the darkness, but he was too exhausted after everything that had happened. He didn't think he could stand further discussion, no matter what it was about, but stupidly, he lay there and thought of how beautiful she was and of how good she had felt and how much he wished she would come back to bed.

Josh missed how Emma had always understood. He wished he could go and see her. Since that was impossible, he did something he never did, he went for a walk for no other purpose than to be left alone, but even here he could not find any respite from his thoughts.

The following day he walked a long way, up beyond the town, away up the hills where the fields gave way to moorland and nothing stirred beyond the rabbits, bobbing grey and white in the fields, the sheep looking strangely at him because they saw so few people, a discarded roofless farmhouse where nettles and long grass had grown inside and out. Then he turned around.

Below him were dozens of small square fields and tiny farms, and then, further over, the little town with its main streets, and further over still, the various pitheads with their turning wheels, and beyond it all the River Wear and Daniel's foundry and the railway which took the coal from the pits. It made him think of the sermon on the mount, where the devil had taken Jesus and shown him all the kingdoms of the world.

He must not hope for better things, no hoarding up of treasures on earth, or temptation there. He must make the best of what he had. He plunged back down the road. It was almost tea time, the end of the back shift; the miners were pouring out of the pits. He was almost home when he saw someone and heard his name shouted. It was Brendan Kinnear.

'Can I have a word with you, Mr Castle?'

Josh ushered him into the vestry. They could not be overheard by anyone in there. The chapel, he had come to realize, was well used, and he was glad of it, there were always meetings going on, classes, people cleaning. It was good but there was no privacy, so sometimes he came in here and closed the door. He liked it, it was quiet and it looked out with its narrow plain window over the scrubby patch of grass to one side of the chapel.

Nobody went there. Only the door from here led to it. Once or twice lately he had gone there to pray and be alone and feel the pale winter sunlight on his face, knowing there would be no interruption, nobody needing anything, nobody to upset his few moments of peace. He ushered Brendan inside and shut the door.

Brendan faltered. Having achieved his object, he quite obviously didn't know what to say. He was black from the pit, but even so Josh asked him to sit down.

'No, no, I don't want to trail coal dust over everything. I should have gone home and then . . . come back.' Brendan stopped there as though they both knew he would not have done anything of the kind, his courage would have failed him.

'I didn't think you'd be at work today,' Josh said.

'It's like they saying riding a horse is – you have to get back up, even when you're scared.'

Brendan didn't look scared. He looked like there was something very much the matter. Josh was ready to reassure him that a good lad like Alec would go to heaven, that everything would be all right.

'I'm a Catholic, Mr Castle, at least I think so.'

'How do you think so?'

Brendan grinned uneasily, his teeth showing white through his black face, his eyes brown like coffee.

'I can recite the Mass in Latin, you know, like other folk do poetry.'

'Ah,' Josh said into the silence that followed.

'I shouldn't be here then, should I? I haven't been to a church much since I was little. My mam died and she had been poorly for a long time.'

'Your father?'

'I don't remember him. Is it all right for me to come here?'

'It's all right for everybody who wants to come here. Sit down, please.'

Brendan sat down, taking off his cap from his thick dark hair as he did so. He was a tall man and looked ungainly in the rather rickety dining chair which was all Josh had for visitors.

'I drink.'

'Yes, I know.'

'Aye, I know you do.'

Brendan regarded his cap with fascination.

'I'm not nice when I'm drunk. I'm not very nice anyway. Alec and me . . .' He stopped there and caught at his breath and then went on steadily, 'We were friends from being bairns. Elizabeth never liked me. I did all sorts of daft things to get her to like me. She was made of better stuff. She liked Alec. I know why she did. Alec was . . . he was the best lad I ever met. He was always nice to me until . . .'

Beyond the window there was a small stone trough which might have contained flowers at one time but now was full of water. The snow had melted, the evening was not yet cold enough for ice, and a small bird sat on the edge, drinking. It was a sparrow, brown with bright black eyes. Brendan had his back to it but Josh could see it clearly.

'He tried to stop me drinking but I wouldn't. I know he came to you. He was going to give up the friendship but I wouldn't stop, and because you had told him that Elizabeth didn't like it. I thought he had everything. I blamed him and Elizabeth because I thought I had nowt.' Brendan stopped there. Josh let him go on. 'Yesterday when the roof came down he pushed me out of the road. Do you know what his last words were, Mr Castle? He said, "You aren't saved." He died for me because he thought I wasn't worthy to go to heaven. He left his wife and bairn because I was . . .'

Brendan stopped again. The little bird had flown away and the light was beginning to go outside.

'I didn't have a drink last night. You can't think how badly

I wanted one after what had happened. Elizabeth's going to hate me forever now.'

'No, she isn't.' Josh sat down in the other chair, close. 'Because you aren't going to tell her.'

Brendan's eyes opened wider.

'What?'

'That was something private between you and Alec. Nobody has to know. And yes, you'll have to live with it, but we can't measure the love people have for us, we can't alter it, bring it on or push it back, it just happens. And think of it like this, Brendan. You must be somebody very special for Alec to love you that much. You didn't ask for anything, there must be a lot of good things about you.'

Brendan shook his head and didn't answer.

'You really don't think I should tell her?'

'No, I don't. It won't help. Much as you think it might, I think you would be wrong. You can come and see me any time you like, you know, you don't have to come to a service, you can just come here. It's always open, except during the night, but the chapel is open then. Try to treat yourself gently.'

Brendan looked surprised. He also, within moments, looked better. He thanked Josh and left. Shortly afterwards there was an apologetic knocking on the door. When he answered, Patience came in.

'Your mother says, if you don't come for your tea, Wes will have eaten all the cake,' she said.

'What a loss that would be,' he said. 'Patience . . .'

'I'm helping your mother clear up,' she said.

She went out, closing the door behind her. He was shocked at what Brendan had told him. What a burden for Brendan to have to carry, and yet what love there must have been between them.

Love. He thought of the young woman who had just gone out. He would never care for her as he had cared for Emma, but, if she would give him the chance, he might love her differently. She didn't seem inclined to do so. He wished she had stayed here with him, just for a little while. Several times lately he had reached for her in bed and she had pretended she hadn't noticed and turned away. He knew only too well that lust was a sin, but was it also lust when he wanted to relate the day's happenings to her, when he had begun to wish they could have a house of their own, when he watched her from the street and saw other men admiring her beauty and thought proudly that she was his? She was not, that was the truth of it.

He longed for her presence, more and more; was getting to the stage where he would have done almost anything for a smile, when she wouldn't even linger in the vestry with him.

Thirty

Emma went to Alec's funeral. She didn't want to go. There were several people she knew would also be present whom she didn't want to see, but there was no excuse for it. Even though she had seen very little of Alec since his wedding, and Elizabeth just once when she brought the baby to see them, she felt the obligation.

'Do you want me to go with you?' Lucy asked. 'I don't like to think of you there by yourself with all your men.'

'What do you mean?'

'Brendan Kinnear, Daniel Swinburne, to say nothing of the minister.'

'Lucy!'

Emma left it as late as she dared, so that she could slide unnoticed in at the back. She imagined what it would have been like had they been married – she would be standing in the pew at the front where his family stood. She could see his golden-haired wife, his mother and two brothers, even his father was there.

Elizabeth Wyness was as thin as a spelk, Emma thought, and the baby cried throughout. Her mother was with her, skinny and plain-faced. Emma couldn't sing for thinking of Alec in the coffin, and his wife and child without him. The chapel was packed, she was lucky to get in at all, and people who were a little late had to stand outside in the bitter wind.

She could see Daniel Swinburne, and his was the only pew where there was nobody else, like he had a nasty disease, but of course it wasn't that, it was just that nobody wanted to stand with the pit owner. Daniel didn't look up, or sing or do anything. Emma couldn't bear it for him, and while they were beginning the service, she couldn't help herself. She got up off the end of her pew and went a little further forward, it was only the pew in front, as though Daniel also did not want to be there, and she slid in beside him. He stared at her for several seconds. Emma ignored him.

After that she sang very loudly, from sheer defiance of everything, until the people around her joined in. When the service was finished, she would have gone straight home except that, as she emerged from the pew before Daniel should turn around and be obliged to speak to her, Brendan, looking pale and unhappy, said, 'There's tea in the schoolroom and I should go. Will you come with me? I don't want to go in by myself.' So she went.

She spoke to Elizabeth and her mother. Mrs Forrest had nothing to say. Elizabeth was perfectly calm. She even asked Emma to take the baby, and Emma deemed it such a compliment that she carried the child outside, people stopping her on the way to speak to her. Emma had not realized that babies were an asset in difficult social situations.

The day had got out. She walked the baby in the small piece of ground which belonged to the chapel. From there you could just see the edge of the fell. And then she remembered that the child didn't have a father any more, and was trying not to get upset when Daniel appeared beside her.

'Why did you do that?' he said, and fixed her with his icy-blue gaze.

Emma kissed the baby's cool soft cheek. It was awful to think that Alec was dead and his baby was left.

'It was nothing,' she said.

'The church was full. People will talk.'

Emma smiled.

'I hand out pints to the pitmen, try to stop them spitting on the floor, sing sentimental songs. They fight outside and curse. My father was a drunk and a gambler. Maybe you should have moved pews when I got there.'

Daniel almost smiled. He turned away, just in case, she thought, it developed into anything recognizable.

'It was kind of you,' he said, and left.

155

Emma stood for a few moments determinedly not crying, and then she went back inside. She could see Josh and Patience standing very close together, talking. She gave the baby back to Elizabeth. Brendan followed her out.

'Are you coming back to the pub?' she asked him.

'I've given it up,' he said.

'If Joshua Castle becomes any more influential we'll be out of business,' Lucy said grimly, as they sat over their fire drinking tea, and Emma reported what there was to report of the funeral. She could not help reflecting on Daniel Swinburne. She was glad she had gone to sit with him, and she liked how he had come to her afterwards and thanked her. He was so upset about Alec, she knew that he felt responsible for all the people who worked for him, but she wished he had stayed for just a little longer.

Daniel could not bear his own company. He could not stand that Alec had died. He went into Newcastle and to a high-class whorehouse where the girls were young and pretty, and spent the night bedding a red-haired girl with a generous body who spoke with a Berwickshire accent. It was a particularly sweet tone, with its almost Scottish burr, particularly when it was soft with endearments in the cool dark reaches of the night. They went through a bottle of whisky together and, as they did so, her accent got thicker and thicker, but it was still decipherable, or did it not matter when you reached that stage? He thought he could have understood what she meant and what she wanted even if she had been speaking in Latin or Hebrew.

Thirty-One

When she got home after the funeral, Elizabeth expected Alec to be there. She wondered whether she would ever get used to the idea. Her mother was still saying that she must give up the house and come to live with her.

'I can't do that. I wish that you would stop asking me,' Elizabeth said. 'I want to stay here.'

'Daniel Swinburne would never allow it.'

'He said he would.' Indeed, he had come to her at the funeral and reassured her and told her that, if it was convenient, he would call and see her the next day.

'Then I shall come and live with you. You can't stay here by yourself,' her mother said.

Elizabeth was horrified. Losing Alec was bad enough. Having her mother there would complete the disaster.

'I'm sorry but you can't,' she said hurriedly. 'I'm going to take in lodgers.'

'Lodgers?' Her mother stared. 'You won't need to do that, surely.'

'Then what am I to live on?'

'You said yourself that Daniel Swinburne had offered to pay—'

'That's for our future, the baby's and mine. I've got no intention of spending it.'

Nor, though she didn't say anything to her mother, did she want to end up married again, simply because she could not afford to be independent. From somewhere, her mother's lonely life echoed. Was that what her mother had thought, left alone with a small child? Had she loved Elizabeth's father so much that he prevented her from marrying again, or was it

157

that he had disgusted her so much that it put her off? They had never talked about it. Whatever. To say yes to a man for financial reasons was not acceptable to Elizabeth, she would find other ways.

In the early evening, Joshua Castle arrived, and when he had said all the right things that the minister should say, he looked at her and added, 'How will you manage?'

Her mother had been persuaded to go home, so she was able to talk freely.

'Mr Swinburne is going to look after me. I can keep the house and there will be a big lump sum, and then I'm going to take in lodgers, but they will have to be good, clean-living men. Have you any suggestions?'

'What about Abraham Finn? He's looking for somewhere.'

Elizabeth approved this. He was a worker in the iron company offices. Very respectable and a good Methodist.

'I shall need somebody else.'

She watched him hesitate.

'What about Brendan?'

Elizabeth looked at him.

'I won't accuse you of trying to be funny, Mr Castle . . .'

'He loved Alec very much. He's upset and he's trying not to drink, but he lives in a house of drunks and he's hurt. He'll go back to it unless somebody helps him.'

Elizabeth didn't like to turn the minister down.

'He – he likes me,' she said.

'Yes, I know, but I think if Brendan had the chance he would be a good honourable man. His regard for you would help, and his love for Alec's memory would prevent him from becoming a nuisance. Would you let me at least suggest it to him?'

She agreed but it was only out of regard for the minister that she did.

Josh was not very surprised when he got home to find Brendan at the vestry.

'I don't want to be a nuisance to you, Mr Castle, I'll just sit here quietly.'

It was about the time that Brendan would normally have gone off to the Ivy Tree, so Josh understood completely, but he was able to say with some satisfaction, 'You're just the man I wanted to see, Brendan, take a seat.'

Brendan looked surprised. He looked even more surprised when Josh outlined the scheme to him.

'I can't do that,' was his first reaction.

'Elizabeth has agreed to it.'

Brendan looked sceptically at him.

'You talked her into it, saving your position, Mr Castle, that's what you did. You're very persuasive like that.'

'And that makes it a bad idea?'

'No, but—'

'It would be good for you, and if Elizabeth had too much to do, which she will have by the time she's sorted out you on shifts, Mr Finn on days in the office and the baby all the time, it will stop her from thinking about Alec every minute of the day. And you'll be able to help her, you see, carrying in coal and doing difficult jobs she can't reach. It's a two-way thing.' Like all the best things, he added silently. 'Why don't you go and see her? Not today, I think she's had enough for now. Maybe tomorrow about this time?'

Brendan smiled.

'Pub-going time?' he said.

'Why not?' Josh said.

'Thank you, Mr Castle. I would call you devious, except for you're a man of the cloth.'

Josh laughed. It was good to see some light in Brendan's eyes. He had thought he would be lost. They would see.

Brendan was in two minds and it was a difficult place to be. He had always wanted to live with Elizabeth, but he had never thought to live with her like this.

'Well?' she said, as he looked around the bedroom.

There were two single beds in it. Brendan had never had a bed to himself before, it seemed strange. Also he was to have the top two drawers of the dresser and even a little bedside table and a brass candleholder and a chair.

159

He thought the idea of having space to himself charming. He went over to the window. It wasn't much of a view, just the yard, the coal house and the lavatory, the little gap leading into the back lane. It was difficult not to be pleased, even grateful, especially when he thought that he had been the cause of Alec's death.

It kept him awake at night. Alec's ghost haunted him but saved him from the pub. Sobriety was interesting only in the mornings, Brendan thought. The rest of the time it was a bloody nuisance and made you think and see too clearly.

'It's lovely.' He wanted to say her first name but didn't dare.

'I've only one thing to say to you, Mr Kinnear. The first time you take a drink, you will leave.'

'I understand that.'

'Good,' she said, and tramped down the stairs, heavy-footed like somebody a lot bigger than she was.

Brendan stood there contemplating the joy of having his own bed, and the torture of not being able to drink beer, and the guilt of being here without Alec, and he followed her down into the big room where she and the baby would sleep. The baby was crying.

'Can I hold him for you?' he offered as she reached for the child.

'In the first place,' Elizabeth said, with a touch of humour, 'he's a girl, and in the second place, what on earth do you know about babies?'

'Nothing, but I never will if I never have anything to do with them. What is she called?'

'Ruth.'

'A pretty name.'

'"Whither though goest, I will go."' Do you know the story?'

'Doesn't everybody?'

She looked surprised.

'"Where thou lodgest, I will lodge,"' Brendan went on, remembering from some lost childhood day. '"Thy people shall be my people, and thy god my god." I always thought it was the best bit of the Bible.'

Elizabeth handed him the child.

'When can I move in?' he asked.

'Any time that you like.'

He had three days of peace before Abraham Finn arrived. Three days of the novelty of having a room to himself, and then it was lost to the smell of Abraham's cabbage breath, his persistent snoring, his turning over and over in bed all night, snuffling like a hound, his sanctimonious piety – was there such a thing? Brendan thought there must be.

The almost funny part was that the woman he had thought he loved was no longer there. It was as though she had gone to the grave with her husband. The Elizabeth he had loved was lost to some sharp shrewish woman he did not recognize. She had no soft word for anyone.

The meals she made were nowhere near as good as Mrs Murphy's. Perhaps, like a lot of other things, food made without love lost its bite and flavour. Somewhere between Alec's death and here, Brendan's appetite had deserted him and there was nothing left to encourage it.

He thought of Mrs Murphy swigging gin and cooking and how colourful those meals had been, the stews golden brown, the meat flaking off its bones, the onions caramel, the potato white and soft. He thought of the drop scones she would make, so light and sweet and thin, for Sunday tea, glistening with butter, and he ached for beer and good food and the pleasure of Alec's company. Somehow there was nothing left but this. He had reached what felt like the desert of his life. He would have given almost anything for one pint of beer.

It was the cleanest house possibly in the whole world, and the meals were perfectly adequate, but Brendan couldn't eat, and with not drinking and not eating, and working harder than he had ever worked, in the hope that he would forget the accident, he began to lose weight. He had to fasten his belt tighter and tighter, putting new holes into it with the end of a kitchen knife.

'Is there something the matter with my cooking, Brendan?' she demanded one evening as he put yet another hole into his belt while she cleared the table. Abraham had gone to the chapel. He led a class meeting. He was respected, he was a Sunday school teacher. He was all the things that Brendan was not.

It took Brendan a great deal of courage to go into the chapel, much more so than going down the pit after what had happened. He felt like an imposter. The chapel was so plain, he noticed as he began to go regularly. It had been built more than a hundred years ago, with six big windows ground and first floor, right beside the road. The pulpit was right in the middle, so that everybody could see the minister, and presumably so that the minister could see them. It was a very light building because of all the windows, and outside in the grounds surrounding it were lilac trees and bigger oak trees and scrubby land. There were stairs leading to the first storey and pews right round it to seat a good many people, and it was just as well because the chapel was full for every service.

He liked to listen to Mr Castle or one of the visiting preachers, and he liked the singing. Sometimes people would get up and sing alone. He thought that must take a lot of nerve. There was also a social aspect to it all but he had not managed that. He kept his head down when he was there and only went because he had to, but after he went to live with Elizabeth it was pleasant to go to chapel and sit with her, and sometimes now she gave him the baby to look after, because Ruth liked him. To his secret joy, she did not like Abraham and cried whenever he touched her. Brendan thought it was possibly Abraham's beard and big booming voice.

'You haven't cleared your plate once since you got here,' Elizabeth said. 'Do you think I have food to waste?'

'I'm just not hungry.'

'Drunks never are,' she said, and she began to carry the plates from the table across to the sink.

Brendan got up and went upstairs and sat down on the bed. He could hear her clattering around in the kitchen, but after a while her footsteps sounded on the stairs and she knocked and came in. She looked straight at him and she said, 'I'm sorry, I didn't mean to say that to you.'

'Why not? It's true.'

'Yes, but I know how hard you are trying, how difficult it is for you. You didn't use to be so skinny. Why don't you come down?'

He shook his head. Elizabeth hesitated and then she said, 'It wasn't your fault. It was the roof, the – the old props.' He thought suddenly that she had been trying to say it for days, not meeting his eyes, and calling him 'Mr Kinnear', as she called Abraham 'Mr Finn'. As though they had not known one another for years.

He couldn't stand it. He had promised Josh he wouldn't tell her, so he got up and hurried past her down the stairs, but she ran after him and while he was searching for his coat in the shadows behind the door she said, 'Don't you go out there and get drunk. Here, hold the baby.' And she ran into the kitchen and came back with the child and thrust it into his arms.

'I'm not fit to be here,' Brendan said.

'Yes, you are. Sit down and hold Ruth while I wash up.'

'Not when Alec's dead. I miss him so much. I miss him.' Brendan knew that it wasn't the right thing to say to Alec's widow, and he had the awful feeling he was going to start to cry, which he had never done in his life, but to be there with her and with Alec's child, knowing that Alec could have been alive and he could have been dead and that it would have been such a small loss, he just wanted to run out. Unfortunately Ruth began to cry, so he was obliged to walk up and down the kitchen floor with her while Elizabeth got on with tidying the scullery, and the moment passed.

Elizabeth only relieved Brendan of the child when Ruth had gone to sleep, and that took a considerable amount of time. She only did it then because she was convinced it was fairly late, and when he promised that he was not going to the Ivy Tree if he went out. It was bitter, he would not be long, she thought.

Abraham came in shortly after that and went to bed. Elizabeth sat down on the settee with the baby to the inside of her, so there was no chance she would fall, and presently she heard a voice saying her name and she came out of sleep with the delicious anticipation of seeing her husband.

'Alec,' she said gladly.

'No, it's just me.' As she sat up she met Brendan's beautiful dark eyes, he was down beside her, his voice so soft and gentle that she had made a mistake.

Disappointment rushed her like a cold draught, and guilt followed because she was glad it was him rather than somebody else.

'I thought . . .'

'I know. I'm sorry.'

Brendan had hair which made him look like a boy, she thought. Alec's hair had been sprightly and ginger and made him the butt of many a joke which he took in good part, it had been one of the nicest things about him. Brendan's hair was also one of the nicest things about him, because it was unruly in a different way, so that she, and possibly many other women, wished to push it back, because it looked as though it was about to cloud his vision. She didn't. She didn't want to touch any man again ever, but she was conscious of the effort.

'It's very late,' Brendan said. 'Would you like me to get down the bed for you?'

'No, no, I can do it.' How personal that would be.

'I'm on night shift next week. Will that be all right?'

It would be invading her personal space at all hours, since they had only the one room downstairs, but since she had agreed to have him there, she nodded and said yes, it would be fine. She had always liked Alec's different shifts, but that was because she had loved him. Having Brendan coming in dirty and hungry at odd hours would be a different matter altogether, needing food and taking off his clothes so that he could wash when nobody else was about.

He took up a lot more space for a start, because he was a much bigger man than Alec had been. Also, they had made arrangements for he and Abraham to wash upstairs, though he wouldn't be able to do that on certain shifts. She had accepted this man into her house, he was paying her very well for the privilege of being there, so she would just have to get used to him.

It had occurred to her of late that Brendan didn't really want to be there, and considering how she had always thought he was much too fond of her, this was an unpleasant surprise. It was one thing to call a man a nuisance, it was another to discover that he had only wanted her because she belonged to somebody else.

Not that she wanted Brendan anywhere near her, but he had turned into somebody sober, slender and well mannered, and therefore it was somehow annoying to discover that he had also, somewhere between Alec's death and here, been silenced, subdued, almost lost. He could sit for hours without speaking. He didn't take part in anything.

She knew then how much she had liked him, his humour and his intelligence. She didn't want to like him now. She didn't want to like any man ever again. She wanted to run away somewhere and hide. Alec's death had robbed Brendan of all his most attractive qualities. She was relieved in one way and sorry in another.

The only time there was any animation about Brendan was around the time when the pubs opened, and unless he went to sit upstairs as though, if he were far enough away from the outside door, it would help, she knew that he went to the chapel. What he did there she wasn't quite sure, but she had had it on good authority from a number of people that that was what Brendan did in the evenings. Not that she had really suspected him of going to the Ivy Tree Hotel to see Emma Meikle, and she was glad of that. It was mortifying to find that you resented that another woman could sing.

Elizabeth found that she liked Emma, and that was strange. She had not seen Emma since the funeral but she knew also that Emma had liked Alec and she wanted to be with people who had liked him so she found, even though she deplored the idea, that she made her way to the back door of the Ivy Tree one Thursday morning three weeks afterwards and was glad to find Emma open the door herself.

She looked surprised but pleased and sat Elizabeth and the baby by the fire and made tea and Elizabeth had been right, this woman who represented all the things she disliked most would talk about her dead husband to her. A lot of other people whom she had regarded as her friends had not done so but Emma thought nothing of bandying Alec's name about the kitchen, almost as though he were still alive, even more so as though she had great respect for somebody she had liked so well. She even said at one point,

'Alec would have been pleased at how well Ruth's doing, wouldn't he? Look how bright she is.'

Emma walked about the kitchen with the baby in her arms after they had drunk their tea and showed her various cupboards and talked to her just as though the baby was any regular person and Elizabeth could not help smiling.

'How's Brendan?' Emma said as she came back with the baby on one hip, practised, Elizabeth noted.

'Very, very sober. Not like himself at all.' Elizabeth found herself being franker with Emma than she had ever been with anyone before. Somehow Emma's kindness encouraged it. 'And do you know what the worst thing about it is – I liked him better before when he drank and when . . .' she didn't say 'when Alec was still alive.'

'It's funny, isn't it? I get all kinds in here and there are a lot that you wish wouldn't drink but when they don't you sort of wish they were the person that they used to be when they did. Is he all right?'

'No,' said Elizabeth, realizing it for the first time, 'I don't think he is. I'm afraid he's going to die.'

Emma shifted the baby, sat down.

'That's just because it's happened once. Alec's death was . . .'

Elizabeth thought it strange but nobody else had said, 'Alec's death' like that, so straightforward that she admired it.

'I don't mean that,' she said, 'It's like since Alec died he no longer wants to be here. I feel like that too but I don't see why Brendan should feel like that.'

166

'Alec was his only friend.'

'I don't see why.'

'I would have thought it was obvious,' Emma said. 'It was because of you.'

'They were always friends. I don't think it had anything to do with me.'

'Elizabeth, Brendan always thought the sun shone from you.'

'Well, he doesn't now,' Elizabeth said, after a deep breath.

'You're at the lowest point in your life. It would be no sort of a man who tried to get you to care for him.'

It was this that Elizabeth remembered when she went home, the way that Emma had respect for Brendan and also how she had mentioned Alec's name over and over, like she was decorating the room with it. It was so dear to Elizabeth and she liked Emma Meikle more so than any of the women at the chapel even though they were all good to her in different ways.

Thirty-Two

Wesley had begun work at the foundry office and was so pleased with it that Josh could not help a degree of satisfaction. He went off whistling each morning and in the evenings Daniel Swinburne's name was always on his lips. Josh had no doubt that Wesley referred to Daniel as 'Mr Swinburne' when he saw him the office, but when he spoke of him it was 'Danny said' this and 'Danny did' that, a familiar term which Josh, remembering how Daniel Swinburne had rebuked him, over Alec Wyness's body, for even the use of his full first name, doubted anybody dared utter it.

Josh was rather jealous that Wesley admired Daniel so much, and was inclined to disparage him, except that it wasn't necessary. After the first few days, Mrs Castle objected to hearing Daniel's name while she ate her evening meal. Since she had been so against the whole idea, Wesley thereafter learned to hold his tongue, though he looked somewhat disappointed, and Josh thought it was a shame to quench the youthful enthusiasm.

After all, half the joy of the day was recounting what had happened, to somebody's interested ears, so when they had eaten, he would ask Wesley all about it. After the first couple of evenings, Wesley would follow him to the chapel and into the vestry, and very often Brendan was there. Wesley seemed to like Brendan, and Brendan was keen to do anything that would take his mind off the Ivy Tree Hotel, and since Brendan knew the men who helped to run Daniel's offices, the two had plenty to talk about.

Josh wasn't entirely happy about having the vestry turned into a meeting place like this, but this was one of the purposes of the chapel, and since it seemed to work its own magic, he let it go on. Very often other men who came to the chapel would hear them talking, be interested and come in, and it soon became like a little club.

Josh found himself with nowhere to go for peace or reflection. He and Patience, Abraham and various other people held classes in the schoolroom in the evenings, and at home Harry and his mother were always about. When his father did come downstairs he still claimed the little study as his, and while Josh longed for solitude, he could not covet the last place that his father had which gave him any status. He just wished that he had somewhere to go for peace, other than the bedroom, and even then he had to share it with Patience. He loved having her there but he would have liked a little time to himself.

It seemed to him that his father came downstairs more and more as the weeks went past, and spent a great deal of his time in the study. He was always writing, so Josh was not very surprised when his father announced that he rather thought he might take on some preaching. His mother was horrified. She had grown used to his father's illness and did not see him any other way.

'He isn't well enough to get up in that pulpit,' she complained to Josh.

'I think he's looking much better, and if he wants to, then I think we should let him.'

'He'll be wanting to go and preach in Newcastle next,' his mother said.

The following Sunday his father did indeed preach at the chapel, and he seemed so much better for doing this. When people encouraged him and told him how they had got so much from it and how wonderful it was to see him up there again, he thereafter began to do a little more work, and on successive Sundays preached at all the chapels which were within a short walking distance. When he had exhausted these, he began again at the beginning. He also would go to people's houses to give comfort and to guide them, and he would help with the activities in the evenings. Very soon Josh got himself a horse, since there was a small stable across the yard, and was able to go much further to preach. He overheard his mother complaining to Patience in the kitchen one evening.

'He thinks he's John Wesley,' she said. 'That horse is dear to keep and takes a lot of work.'

Josh had a quiet smile over this, but he could get a lot further on horseback.

One night when he came back very late and everybody had gone to bed, he found that when he went upstairs, his wife was not asleep. She turned over as soon as he walked into the room. He put down the candle.

She sat up in bed with a sigh.

'I want to go home to my parents.' And she burst into tears.

Surprised at both her news and her reaction, he sat down on the bed and tried to comfort her.

'Please don't go,' he said. 'I know things have been very difficult, but if you stay here I will try and make things better.'

'I don't think I want to stay here any more. I can't stand it. I want my mother.'

'Why don't you write and ask her to come here?'

'Where would we put her, in the stable with that wretched horse?'

'You're ashamed of us,' he said.

She dried her eyes on a scrap of a handkerchief she had taken from under her pillow and didn't look at him.

'I haven't told them how poor we are.'

'There's nothing to be ashamed of in that.'

'There is for me. My parents judge things differently. I want to go home. I want my old bedroom and my friends and . . . We haven't exactly been happy here.'

'I'm sorry.'

'If I ask her, my mother will send me the money so that I can go home for a while.'

Josh could see that she had made up her mind.

'By all means go if you wish,' he said.

He tried to sleep, rather unsuccessfully, and from the number of times she turned over, Patience had the same problem.

Josh did not say anything to his parents during the days which followed, but Patience turned away from him in bed every night, and, during the day, though she spent a great deal of time at the chapel, he thought she did it to get away from his mother's questioning gaze.

The days dragged themselves past until it was almost two weeks, and then she came to him in the vestry and said, 'I . . . I had a letter from my mother this morning and she has sent me the money to go home.'

Josh was beginning to feel quite sick. Bristol was a long way and he remembered the easier life, the luxury.

That evening Patience told his mother and father that she was going home for a while, and they received the news with silence. Josh went back to the vestry and hid there until it was late, but when he went back to the house, his father came to him and said simply, 'Why is Patience leaving you?'

'She finds it very hard to live like we do.'

'Don't they live like this?'

'No, they're very prosperous, very . . .'

'It must have been difficult for her here.'

'Yes, I think it was.'

Josh put her on the train that very day. He did not blame her for wanting to go. His mother was casting black looks at her and his father went off to the chapel to get out of the way. Patience said nothing. She looked relieved when she got on the train. She didn't even look back as he stood waiting while the train pulled away and then got smaller and smaller, before it finally turned the corner and was lost to his sight.

It was doubly difficult to go back and behave as though nothing was the matter, and the moment he walked into the house, his mother came out of the kitchen and said, 'She went, then?'

'Yes.'

'You couldn't use that . . . charm of yours to stop her.'

He wasn't sure whether his mother was being sarcastic, and he knew then that the people in the village would judge him, talk about him, say that his wife had left him and it was his fault.

171

'There was nothing I could do,' he said.

'Perhaps you'd already done everything,' she said, and made him feel even more at fault.

The news soon spread all over the small town that the preacher's wife had left him. The rumour was that the Methodists, being mean, small-minded people, had treated the lass badly, and that he had knocked her about and she had run off with another man. Emma didn't believe it but she hated that so many people were willing to do so. She held off going to him for several days. In fact she had never intended going anywhere near, but in the end, because the town was rife with gossip, she waited until a very wet tea time well before the pub opened, and hopefully when other people would be preoccupied at home, and made her way to the chapel.

She had judged it correctly, there was nobody about except a seated figure in the vestry, writing. He looked up when he heard her. Emma listened to the rain bouncing off the roof and let down her hood, and then she saw his face and knew that she should not be there. If anybody found out, he would be completely condemned.

He looked awful, she thought, tired, skinny and defeated.

'Emma.' He smiled.

She went into the room and closed the door.

'I know I shouldn't be here—'

'If you've got a problem—'

'It's not me, it's you. Everybody is talking about you. Where has Patience gone?'

'Back to her parents.'

'But why?'

He put down his pen.

'I suppose she couldn't stand it any more. Who could blame her?'

Emma subsided into a chair, her coat heavy with rain.

'Why now?'

'I don't know,' he said, looking down. 'Her parents have a great deal of influence and money. You can do anything

172

when you're like that, and she is their only child. She told me that she would come back but . . .'

'You don't expect her to.'

'Why would she? She has nothing here.'

'Why did you marry her?'

He smiled.

'I think it was because I wanted her in my arms. Isn't that disgusting?'

'It isn't disgusting at all,' Emma said, not wanting to hear this but glad that at least he was being honest with her.

'Isn't it?' He looked wildly at her. 'When I loved you so very much? I've behaved so ill to you both. She doesn't want me any more. Whatever can I do?'

Emma looked at him and it was in some ways like seeing him for the first time.

'I don't think you ever loved me as you loved Patience.'

'What does that mean?'

'Haven't you ever thought about it? You went and left me but you couldn't keep your hands off her.'

'That's not true.'

'Oh, please, Josh, stop being the minister. If you had wanted to bed me you could have . . .'

'That's not love!'

'Isn't it? Is that you speaking or your church? You wanted her.'

'I was upset. I was—'

'You're hiding behind the man who helps other people with their problems. I think the truth of the matter is that you knew very well for a long time that Patience was the right woman for you—'

'She burned your letters.'

Emma was silenced for a few moments.

'She did?'

'Yes. I didn't know you'd moved. I didn't know what was happening.'

'So Patience is to blame for the fact that your love for me was such a fragile thing that you left me and then married another woman. Is that right?'

173

He said nothing.

'I waited for you,' she said. 'The truth of the matter is that you loved your church better than you loved me, but when it came to Patience, your natural instincts were stronger. Isn't that right? Are you going to blame her forever for what happened?'

'I don't blame her!'

'You hypocritical bastard,' she said. 'I wish I hadn't spent two years waiting for you. For goodness' sake, have the decency to admit that you love her.'

He stood there with his head down for so long that she almost walked out, and then he said in a low voice, 'Yes, you're right. I tried not to love her. I found her frivolous and foolish and overindulged and I was so conceited that I thought she was beneath me. I was ashamed to have married her, so when I found out about the letters, it was easy to blame her for something which was my own doing. I want her so much that I can hardly breathe.'

'She must love you very much too, to have put up with the way that you have treated her. You don't deserve her. I shall never spend another second regretting you. You are a complete and utter bastard.' And Emma walked out.

Josh went on writing. The writing had taken on a volition of its own. It was the only thing between himself and the misery, as though the writing had provided a kind of wall which held it off. He didn't go back to the house for anything to eat, and it was much later when he finally looked up and saw his mother standing in the doorway.

'What did that Emma Meikle want?'

'Nothing.'

'Is she the reason that Patience left you? Have you been carrying on with her?'

Josh held on to his temper and smiled slightly.

'No,' he said.

'People will say it if she comes around here. Whatever was she thinking of? You're the minister, you couldn't marry rubbish like her. You should never have let Patience go. You were never nice to her,' his mother said, 'and if you are going

174

to go on seeing that publican's daughter, you can kiss goodbye to your ministry as well. Word will soon get round.
Everybody is gossiping and you have no more sense than to
let that woman come here—'

'I didn't ask her to.'

'People say you're having an affair with her, and the truth
of the matter is that I wouldn't put it past you. You've
always wanted her. You never had any judgement in these
matters, and now you've let a wonderful woman leave you.
I don't understand why she's left you, but I will say this.
Your father has always been kind to me, and if a man is
kind to his wife, she doesn't walk out like that. You're a
disgrace, you—'

'Why, Mrs Castle, I didn't know you were in here,' Brendan
said, as he opened the door.

She turned around, looked at him, and then she left.

'I didn't mean to butt in. I could have come back.'

'No, no,' Josh said, and then he couldn't say anything else.
His throat closed.

'You all right?' Brendan said, without ceremony, as he
closed the door.

'Fine,' Josh said.

Brendan put a whole pile of money, which he had been
carrying in his fist, down on the little desk in front of Josh.

'What's that?'

'I was saving it, like, for a rainy day.' Brendan nodded at
the wet windows. 'It's for you. You can go down to Bristol
and get your wife back.'

'Oh Brendan, I can't take it,' Josh said gently, pushing the
money at him. 'She left me because she didn't want to be
with me. It won't make any difference if I go chasing down
to Bristol. But I thank you for the idea and for thinking about
me.'

'What are you going to do, then?'

'I'm going to write my sermon,' Josh said.

It was such a relief for Patience when she got off the train and
into her father's arms. She tried not to cry but it didn't work.

He handed her into the carriage and drove her swiftly home, and it was only when she saw the gravity of her mother's expression that she was sorry for what she had done. They didn't question her. They had her luggage brought in, not nearly as much luggage as she had gone with, settled her down before the drawing-room fire with tea, and it was not until her mother had seen her drink at least one cup of tea and attempt to eat a sandwich that she said to her, 'Patience, what is going on?'

'I've come home,' she said brightly. 'It's just a visit. I wanted to see you.'

They looked at each other. They told her that that was wonderful, that they were glad she had come back.

Having successfully got away from Josh, Patience promptly missed him. That first evening, left alone with her mother – she thought her father went off so that they could talk – her mother coloured slightly and said, 'Did your husband do something to you?'

'Yes,' Patience laughed awkwardly, 'he broke my heart. The truth of the matter is that I should not have married him.' And she told her mother how she had admitted to Josh that she had destroyed his letters from Emma, and that he was still in love with the other girl.

'I deceived him, and you, and myself as well. I didn't recognize the woman who would go so far, envy and jealousy and all those awful things I had always told myself I would never feel. I did and they bettered me,' she said. 'I didn't know what people would do to reach what they wanted.'

Her mother tried to be sympathetic and understanding, but Patience could see that she was very shocked. Finally she said, 'I still think that if he had not cared for you a great deal, he would never have married you. I can see that the marriage didn't work. If it was never consummated, it could be annulled.'

It was Patience's turn to be embarrassed. She thought of that early morning after Alec had died, and how upset Josh had been, and of making love in the early light, the intensity, the need, but it had not been love, and she could not have gone on in such a way.

'They treated me like a servant,' she said. 'I scrubbed floors and picked up clothes after those wretched boys because they couldn't afford a maid, and Mrs Castle was horrible to me.' And then she thought how often Josh's mother had told her how pleased she was that he had married her, how Wes said that her cooking and baking were 'streets ahead' of his mother's, and how she would sit upstairs with Mr Castle when he hadn't been so well, and how grateful he was to her.

'And now I miss them,' Patience said, and she cried.

She missed taking classes in the evenings, and the Sunday school, and all the things which Josh had planned for the summer, an outdoor Bible camp for all the people of the circuit who wished to attend. She thought how much she had been looking forward to that.

'It's easier to be understanding at a distance,' her mother said.

Her parents kept up the pretence that she was only home for the summer, and even though the days passed and nothing changed, they talked brightly to other people of their son-in-law, especially those who had known him.

Her mother took her shopping and to see friends in other cities, to take her mind off things, she thought, and Patience could not believe that she had ever lived this overindulged life. She felt guilty when the new maid, Eva, picked up and tidied after her, and she was bored at the dinners her parents held. She also realized that, as a married woman, she held no interest for young men, and they would not talk to her for any length of time.

She wondered how Elizabeth Wyness was getting on, how big the baby was, and if Brendan had gone back to drink and had to leave. She wondered whether Josh's father was getting better, and how his mother was coping with the extra work, but most of all she thought of the way that Josh had looked at her when she left him on the station platform, his face totally devoid of expression, and of all those times when he had come home late and tired after comforting a bereaved family or listening for hours to somebody's problems and she had turned away from him in bed.

The summer seemed to get longer and longer. Josh wrote her very polite letters which she fell on as they arrived, escaping into the garden to sit under the trees to read them alone. The joy of it was that they all wrote to her. Mrs Castle wished she had never gone, Josh was a bad husband and a worse son and she didn't blame Patience for leaving him, Mr Castle wrote that he was feeling much better and taking on more and more duties every week, Wes wrote long boring letters about the goings on at the ironworks, and Harry, obviously compelled by his mother, said he hoped she was having a lovely time in Bristol, it was always raining in Durham.

The sentence went through her mind and made her think of how grey the hills were in the rain and how, since it was August, the heather would be a purple lake beyond the town, the stream below the houses would be brown and running slow over big flat stones, and Josh would be hiding from his family in the vestry, watching the sparrows bathing in the little stone trough beyond the tiny window.

Did he miss her? He didn't say that he did. Neither did he say that he wanted her to come back. He wrote about the general doings of people, but there was no life to it, no intimacy, nor had she really expected any.

That summer saw his father's recovery. The people called it a miracle, but Josh could see that what his father had needed was rest and care. It was much easier with two of them doing the work, but he was terrified that he would have so little to do that he would think about Patience all the time. On the other hand, he needed to let his father do as much work as he felt able. His father even came into the vestry in the evenings and to the various activities at the chapel, so that Josh felt he had no responsibility or privacy anywhere, and he had to be careful not to contradict the ways and ideas which Mr Castle implemented.

The autumn came. The days were shorter and cooler. Josh worked harder and harder, doing things which he was not sure were necessary, just to keep from thinking about what a mess he had made of his personal life. One October morning his father came to him in the vestry and he felt a degree of irritation. His father was so well by now it was difficult to think he had ever been ill. He sat down on the rickety chair across the desk and said, 'I've come to take back my job. It is mine.'

Josh looked at him.

'It's official,' his father said before he could speak. 'I had a letter this morning.'

'Where am I going?' was all Josh said.

'I don't know. I know where you should be going, to Bristol to talk to Patience. She's been gone too long. You should have gone before now. A minister whose wife has left him is a very questionable asset, and in a small town like this, it won't do. You should go there and try to win her back. Failure to do so could cost you your career.'

Josh looked at him.

'You sent me to the Matthews' family deliberately, didn't you? You never intended that I should take up the kind of work you did.'

His father looked straight back at him.

'Any reasonably intelligent man could do what I do. You could do a lot more. It was one of the most disappointing days of my life when you came back here. I told them over and over I didn't want you here. Filial duty was not the point. You never fitted, not really.' His father smiled at him. 'You proved it by marrying a girl who could not live here. You did it on purpose, even if you didn't know it at the time. You weren't born for this. You were meant for a different life, and if you have half as much courage as I think you have, you'll go forward and try to gain it.'

'You knew I wanted Emma.'

'I remember the day you met. I was so angry with myself for having taken you to Mrs Richmond's. Emma is a lovely woman but she was never going to be a wife for you. You chose the right woman in the end.'

'She doesn't love me. She loves this – this person who thinks he's so clever and knows better than everybody else and tries to manoeuvre people about, and he thinks he's more intelligent and—'

179

'That is who you are.'

'It isn't.'

'Josh, everybody can see it but you. Our church will prosper if we have the right leaders, but if those men don't come forward to take the responsibility, whatever are we to do?'

'There must be lots of people capable of it.'

'And if they are all hiding in little pit towns?' his father said, smiling.

'I'm not hiding.'

'What kind of a man lets his wife leave him like that?'

'She's coming back.'

'Nonsense. You have to go to her.'

'How can I do that?'

'Pride is a great sin,' his father said. 'Don't you love her?'

'Yes, but I don't feel entitled to her.'

'Because she was socially above you? Josh, that's nonsense. She's proved how much she cares for you by coming here, and you . . . if you want her now, you have to go and tell her. Otherwise you will never get her back. Things have to change.'

'What if I can't come back here ever?'

'If it's meant to be, it will, but sometimes you have to go and grab what is yours.'

'And if you're ill again?'

'Each man has his own destiny.'

Josh hesitated, looked down at the sermon he had been writing.

'What does my mother say?'

'She's packing your bags.'

Josh left him there and went slowly back into the house and up the stairs, and there, as his father had said, his mother had a suitcase open on the bed and was arranging his clothes in different piles. She looked up.

'You talked to your father?'

'You really think I should go?'

'That poor girl,' his mother said. 'I don't know . . . Men are supposed to have the brains. How much longer is she supposed to wait? I said at the time you should never have come back here. I . . .'

She turned away, fussing about socks. Josh couldn't believe it. His mother was crying over him. He went over and kissed her on the cheek and she moved past him, saying, 'And none of that either. You have more suits than any man I ever met. Leave me to do this. Go and do something useful.'

That night, when it was late, when Emma was tidying up in the bar, she heard a noise in the doorway behind her.

'We're closed.'

He didn't move. She looked up. It was Josh.

'Why, if it isn't the preacher,' she said.

He moved further inside and shut the door.

'You won't do what's left of your reputation any good coming here like this,' Emma said. 'My takings are down a long way.'

'I'm leaving,' he said.

'Do you know, I think I heard it somewhere before. You were right. We were never meant to be together.' She looked at him over her broom handle. 'So you're going to Bristol to ask her if she'll have you back?'

He looked straight at her.

'I love her, Emma.'

'I hope things turn out well for you.'

'Thank you.'

Thirty-Three

Daniel heard the noise from his office, shouting at first and louder shouting and then the dull noises of a fight. As he opened the office door, Wesley Castle and one of the other clerks, Melvin Wright, were already on the floor, papers everywhere, a chair knocked over, and the other men in the office standing back, looking awkward and embarrassed. Nobody, strangely enough, Daniel thought, was trying to stop them.

Daniel pulled Wesley, who seemed to be having the better of it, off Melvin, and when they were both on their feet he said, 'My office.'

They stood there, rather shamefacedly, as he picked up the chair and the other men began picking up the papers, and then they followed him inside. Daniel closed the door.

'What is going on?' he said.

Melvin looked towards the window. Daniel tried not to think what Joshua Castle would say when he found out that his brother had been fighting at work. Wesley's family hadn't wanted him there in the first place, Daniel knew.

'Wesley?' Daniel prompted him.

Wesley looked down.

'You tell me or you walk out this office without a job.'

Wesley looked at him.

'He called my brother names. Josh didn't do any of those things.'

Melvin glanced at him and sneered.

'Everybody knows he did.'

'Did what?' Daniel said, turning his gaze on Melvin.

'Had it off with the barmaid at the Ivy. That's why his woman left.'

Daniel had already heard the rumours.

'It's not up to you to spread evil talk,' he said.

'It's true.'

'You don't know. It's very easy to destroy a man's reputation, Melvin. That makes you just as dishonourable as the things you accuse him of. And to speak in such a way of Miss Meikle is appalling.'

Melvin looked blankly at him. Daniel cursed his only form of education, his father. He was beginning to sound like him, and he had always taken care not to say things which these men might not understand.

'You cannot know whether it's true, so you shut up,' Daniel said. 'That's the right thing to do. One more word out of you on this matter, Melvin, and you go back to your mother and tell her you don't have a job. Do you hear?'

'Yes, sir.'

'Out, then,' Daniel said. 'Not you, Wesley.'

Melvin closed the door. Daniel looked into Wesley's eyes.

'You don't say anything to anybody about this, and I'll tell the others they are not to. You start a fight in my office again and I'll take a stick to you. Do you understand?'

'I didn't start it,' Wesley protested.

'Are you arguing with me?'

'Josh has never hurt anybody in his life.'

'Don't be naïve. And don't pretend you don't understand when you do. Intelligence is the greatest luxury of all. Don't abuse it. Now go back in there and do some work, it's what you get paid for.'

Wesley didn't quite slam the door. Daniel had to fight back the inclination to go after him and clip him round the ear for it.

Emma did not know when the rumours had started and she did not know how. All she knew was that her public room had emptied within a week. She cursed herself for having gone to Josh at all, somebody must have seen her and got ideas. She had not understood how precarious the standing of either of them was in the community, but it was such a small

183

town and people had prejudices, and men especially had prejudices against women they even just thought might be loose-
moralled, and once you had a loss of esteem like that, she
doubted it could be regained.

On the Monday evening, therefore, she and Lucy sat over
the fire in the big empty room and tried to consider what to
do.

'We're going to have to leave, just as we did when Father
was alive,' Lucy said. 'I never liked the place anyway.'

'We haven't got the money to leave, Luce,' Emma said.
'We haven't finished paying off the debts yet. We're living
from week to week. I won't be able to pay Daniel the rent. I
shall have to go and tell him.'

Lucy sat back slightly from the fire, and her countenance
was pale in spite of it.

'If we can't leave and we can't stay, what are we to do?
We can always go on the street, of course . . .'

'That isn't funny.'

'It wasn't meant to be funny. I've had two offers to go up
the back alley beyond the butcher's. So much for being an
old maid. What do you think it's like being an old whore?'

'Whores don't get old, they die of nasty things first.'

'Oh, lovely,' Lucy said, but they looked at each other and
smiled encouragingly. 'I tell you what, we'll do a moonlight
flit. We should be good at it, we've done it so often.'

Emma wanted to put off going to tell Daniel, but there was
no point. It was not as though things were going to get any
better, so the following morning, not long before midday, she
went to the Delight, hoping that Daniel had seen fit to go to
one of his other offices that morning, or better still, none of
them at all, so that she wouldn't have to face him. He was
there.

One of the men in the outer office saw her inside without
a word. Daniel got up as the door closed. Emma didn't give
him a chance to speak. She said quickly, 'I can't pay you the
rent.'

'Well, and isn't that a surprise.'

Daniel was not in a good mood. Emma didn't blame him.

'I will send you it.'

He looked at her.

'From where?'

'From wherever we get to.'

'You're leaving?' She obviously had surprised him now.

'There's nothing else for it. The gossip has emptied the bar. Josh is going to Bristol of course, but it's too late, the damage is done.'

'He's really going?'

'His wife and his parents-in-law live there.'

'Don't worry about the rent.'

'I promise I will send it,' she said.

There were not many customers that evening, but some of the diehards still came to the pub, and for once the piano player had turned up, so Emma sang. While she was singing, she saw Daniel come in at the back of the room and stand there, listening as they all did in the quietness, as though he had known she was singing 'The Oak and the Ash and the Bonny Ivy Tree'.

He didn't linger. She didn't expect him to. She wished he had, but it was no more than a wish. The following night he turned up again, and so did several other men, and after that he was in every night, and the pitmen and the foundry men followed him, so that within a fortnight, Emma's takings were almost back to normal. She wanted to thank him but she didn't dare. He was always gone before the last song, so it was nothing like it had been. She thought of him in the bitter weather in that great barn of a house, alone, and she had to stop herself from going to him, she wanted to so much.

Thirty-Four

'Mr Finn has asked me to marry him,' Elizabeth announced the first Sunday in November.

It was almost midday and she had come back from chapel and was making the dinner. She was so organized, Brendan thought. She peeled the vegetables and made up the Yorkshire pudding mix before she went out, and she timed the beef perfectly. He was inclined to tell her that she could stay and socialize and have a cup of tea after the service, as other people did, instead of dashing back here to take the meat from the oven, that he would stay and look after the dinner, but she would have been horrified. Men didn't do things like that, and besides, she expected him to go to chapel with her and the baby and Abraham.

Brendan was a lot less enamoured of the whole idea than he had been. It was the magic of Josh's presence that had held him there. Now, increasingly, Josh's father would take the service. It was not the same. It shouldn't have mattered, but somehow it did. He had stopped going to the vestry in the early evening, because very often Mr Castle was there too, and the activities at the chapel bored Brendan.

He had thought that not drinking would get easier but it didn't. Every time he passed a pub, he would linger for the smell of tobacco fumes and beer, and often now he would stand outside the Ivy Tree and listen to the sweet sound of Emma Meikle's voice. It meant more to him than any amount of singing in chapel of a Sunday morning. He missed Emma and he missed the beer more and more.

Abraham had stayed at the chapel that morning. He would time his coming back for the moment Elizabeth put the food on the table. He was never any help, nor did she expect him to be.

She was busying about the house when she told Brendan of the proposal. She didn't look at him.

'He's asked you to marry him?'

'It'll mean you have to move out, of course.'

'You've said yes then?'

'I told him I would think about it.'

Brendan stood in front of her as she came back from putting the Yorkshire puddings into the oven. Her face was flushed and she had a cloth in her hands.

'You love Abraham Finn?'

If she said she did, he would go upstairs and pack his bags and be gone in ten minutes.

'He's a good man.'

'He's old!'

'He is not old.' Elizabeth dodged past him.

'Why?' Brendan said.

She didn't answer, tried to walk round him, and he moved into the way.

'Will you not do that?' she said.

'Why?'

'Because he's good.'

'Good?'

'Yes.'

'You mean he's not a beer-swilling Irish Catholic?'

'He's never taken a drink in his life.'

'I don't call that a reason to marry a man who is twenty years older than you, snores loudly and smells of cabbage.'

'You're offensive now, Brendan.'

'I'm offensive? He's repulsive. Do you really see yourself in bed with him?'

'Don't be disgusting,' she said. 'He's old, you said.'

'You think he won't want that? You're deluding yourself.'

She didn't answer. Brendan stood and watched as she prodded vegetables and made up gravy. The meat sat on the table, awaiting the rest of the dinner. Usually at that point she would lift the meat with a big fork and put the bread in the hot fat,

187

tear it in half and hand half to him and eat the rest. And they would smile conspiratorially at one another before Abraham came back. But today she didn't offer. It was just as well, Brendan had lost his appetite.

When she had set the table and everything was ready and she had gone round his unmoving figure a dozen times, she said, 'I am going to marry him.' And he understood why. Abraham was as unlike Alec as he could be, and it was all she could bear.

Abraham came in at that point and they sat down at the table and Abraham talked to her of people at the chapel, who was saved and who wasn't, about backsliders and fools and those on whom God had turned his back because they weren't worth saving, and Brendan looked down at his dinner and knew then that he could never be saved, that Alec had died for nothing. He would go to hell and Abraham and Elizabeth would go to God, and there was nothing that could be done. He was bored. He was lonely and he was sick and tired and fed up of hearing about the goings on at the chapel.

When they had finished eating, Abraham was going back to the chapel to a meeting. Elizabeth took Brendan's cold, untouched dinner away from him without a word. While she was washing up, Ruth began to cry.

'Will you get the baby, Brendan?' she called from the pantry.

Brendan walked up and down with the baby in his arms until finally, as Elizabeth emerged, Ruth went to sleep. He put her down into her cot and then he went upstairs.

After a little while, Elizabeth followed him there.

'You're leaving now, aren't you?'

'You knew I was.'

'I'm not trying to insult Alec's memory by marrying again—'

'I never said you were. There's no reason why you shouldn't wed anybody you choose.'

'It won't be for a long while yet. Brendan, you can't go back to the Murphys.'

'I'll be pleased to, if they'll have me,' he said.

'You'll drink.'

188

'Aye, I probably will. You shouldn't worry about it. You did your best.'

He thought about the nights, coming and going in the darkness of the last couple of months, coming back to the fire in the middle of the night, and a meal and hot water and her sweet presence. He thought it was the most precious time of his whole life.

And, he thought, Joshua Castle was right. You can't make people love you. It's a gift. Alec hadn't died because Brendan wasn't saved, he had died because he loved Brendan and had been trying to push him out of the way, and because, like all other men, he did not think he would die himself.

'You're not a good man,' she said. 'You never were.'

'That's true,' Brendan said.

'Are you going, then?'

'Aye, I'm off.'

'Well go!' she said and flounced out, quite unlike her usual calm self. She slammed the door after her and it awoke Ruth, who began to scream. Brendan took his bag downstairs and dumped it by the door and, since she hadn't taken the child out of her cot, he did so. Almost immediately the baby's cries ceased.

'You have a way with bairns,' Elizabeth said.

When the baby quietened, he put her into Elizabeth's arms and went to the door again, and as he did so, Elizabeth started to cry so very softly that, if he had not seen her shuddering shoulders, he would have gone. She put the baby down. Brendan went back to her and he got hold of her and when she tried to turn her face away he kissed her. She protested, 'Don't do that, Brendan,' but she had stopped crying. In fact she had her hands on the front of his shirt in a way that couldn't fail to encourage him, and Brendan revised all of his ideas in the seconds when her mouth began to return the kiss. If he had nothing else in his life, he had had this.

And then she reacted as though he had scalded her, let go, stepped back abruptly, and that was when Abraham walked in. If only he had timed it five seconds sooner, Brendan thought, everything would have been different. As it was,

Brendan smiled on Elizabeth, now at a very safe distance, and he said, 'Thank you for everything.' And then he moved past Abraham without looking at him, picked up his bag and left.

That night was a homecoming. Mrs Murphy had had a clear-out while he wasn't there, which was to say that half the family had left, so in fact he had a whole bedroom to himself, something of a revelation. It was a big bedroom and there was nothing in it except a new bed and a chair and clean new bedlinen. Brendan couldn't believe it.

'What happened?'

'I came into some money,' Mrs Murphy said, smiling. 'And our Teresa finally got wed and our Connor found himself a lass over at Cornsay and all of a sudden there's nobody here. Could you eat something, Brendan? I'm still cooking for ten and everybody's gone.'

They sat down at the kitchen table and Mrs Murphy automatically gave him beer and Brendan took a sip of it and he thought it was almost as good as Elizabeth Wyness's kiss.

'It's nectar, Ma,' he said.

He ate the steak and kidney pie she gave him and then he went to the Ivy Tree Hotel and Emma was singing and Brendan could not understand why he had ever gone away. The beer went down, though not as fast as it used to, just at a moderate pace, and she sang all the songs he had loved so well, and she sang them with a feeling he had not noticed before, and at the end of the evening he went to her and thanked her and she said how nice it was to see him there, but had he fallen out with Elizabeth? He told her that, on the contrary, everything was fine, and even though he could see Emma didn't believe him, she nodded and smiled and accepted it.

Thirty-Five

Josh was enjoying the solitude in the vestry, possibly for the last time. His family had tactfully let him get on with it, and for once there was nobody about, it being a Monday tea time. He was leaving the following day. He wandered through into the chapel, which for once was empty, and looked about, wondering whether he would ever be there again, and he heard a noise in the doorway. He turned around. It was Elizabeth.

'Mrs Wyness.'

'Mr Castle.' She didn't go on for a few moments. 'The rumour is that you're leaving.'

'I am, yes. I had hoped to say goodbye to everybody but . . .' He tried to make a joke of it. 'My father is very keen to get rid of me.' He moved closer. She had been crying, he could see how moist her eyes were. 'Come through into the vestry.'

The fire burned in there. He closed the door and as he did so a wave of regret flooded over him. He wanted to be here among these people so very much. He knew he could help them, they needed him.

'Abraham has asked me to marry him.'

'Really?' Josh tried not to look shocked. Abraham was a good man but set in his ways and rather dull. Josh felt a flash of guilt. He had sent Abraham to live with Elizabeth.

'I told Brendan that he must leave. I'm afraid he's gone back to Mrs Murphy's house and the Ivy Tree Hotel.'

Where else would he go? Josh thought.

'I did it on purpose,' Elizabeth said, and sat down heavily in a little chair before the fire. 'I was afraid.'

191

'Afraid of what?' Josh didn't like to tower over her, so he sat too.

'Of myself. Brendan is . . . is . . .'

'Somebody you might care about?' Josh ventured.

She looked at him.

'A pit house is a very close place,' she said.

'You love Brendan?'

Elizabeth blushed so much that it was painful to watch, and in the few moments that passed, Josh realized that Elizabeth loved Brendan as he loved Patience. There was nothing pure about it, it was all about need and touch, and it was about joy, the joy of living, something that was of the heart rather than of the head.

'What I felt for Alec was love. This is . . .' She smiled. 'Brendan doesn't eat my dinners.'

'Elizabeth, Brendan watched you marry Alec while he loved you both. Now you're asking him to watch while you marry another man.'

'I've always been afraid of him,' she said, getting up in agitation. 'He's all those things that can disrupt everything.'

This, Josh thought, was Elizabeth's childhood speaking, her mother had been so hurt that she never ventured beyond her neat rooms, orderly shop and perfectly contained child. Elizabeth had married Alec because he made her feel safe, so she could carry on being the person her mother wanted and needed her to be.

'I've always stayed away from him,' she said. 'He's the very opposite of me and of everything I've been brought up to believe in. My mother didn't like Alec but she knew he was a good man. There's something about Brendan that won't or can't be held or restrained and it frightens me. I don't know why. It isn't as if he's done anything wrong. He's . . . he's good with the baby and kind and funny and . . .'

'You want him?'

Elizabeth looked at Josh.

'That isn't proper.'

'Perhaps you have to take a chance, reach out, gamble a little.'

192

Elizabeth's face changed at the idea of gambling.

'Try for a little more,' Josh urged her. 'Don't run for safety. I don't think it's going to make you happy.'

'He lights the room,' she said. 'Isn't that foolish?'

'Why don't I go and rescue him from himself before he drinks too much?'

'Would you?' Her face was bright, eager. 'I'll collect Ruth from my mother and go and get the tea ready.'

She hurried away. Josh looked around the vestry. He had thought to gain a little peace there on his last night, but this was much more important.

Emma was not singing when Josh got there. He was relieved. He couldn't even see her. Daniel Swinburne was standing in the shadows beside the far wall and Brendan was sitting near the front of the room with beer on the table. It wasn't late, indeed the pitmen were still coming in. Some of them looked hard at him but they didn't say anything. Josh made himself walk through them to reach Brendan. Lucy, Emma's sister, looked scathingly at him before he got there.

'Come to pluck the brand from the burning, Mr Castle?'

'Miss Meikle. How are you?'

'I can do without you in my bar, chasing away my customers. We put up with you preaching the evils of drink. I don't see why we have to have it here.'

'I just want a word with Brendan.'

'The best thing you can do is to leave us all alone,' she said, and swept away from him.

Brendan looked up rather shamefacedly as Josh reached him, but Josh could see a spark of anger too and he was glad of that.

'Let me be,' Brendan said.

'May I sit down?'

'No, you bloody can't,' Brendan said, but he said it mildly. Josh sat.

'Elizabeth came to see me,' Josh said.

'I don't want to hear about it. I can't go on being the man that Elizabeth Wyness's husband died to save,' Brendan said.

'I'm never going to be a Methodist, Mr Castle, I wasn't made that way. You've been kind to me and I'm sorry I hear you're leaving, but all that religious stuff . . . I don't want it. I'm not going to give up who I am to please a woman I can never have.'

'And if you could have her?'

'Even then I wouldn't.'

Josh sat back in his chair.

'Well, she's gone back to make the tea and she's expecting you, so it's up to you. I don't think Elizabeth really wants you to change, Brendan, I think she just wants you to eat your meals occasionally.'

Brendan stared.

'There's no hurry,' Josh said. 'You finish your drink before you go.' And he got up and strolled out.

Abraham went back to the chapel after he had eaten his tea, but not before Elizabeth told him that it was very kind of him to ask but she couldn't marry him. Abraham looked dismayed and she felt sorry, but when the house was empty she immediately felt much better.

The baby went to sleep and shortly after that there was a knock on the door. She half-expected it to be Brendan, but when it was, she couldn't think how to breathe.

'You'd better come in,' she said, and then, because she couldn't think of anything to say, she said, 'Are you comfortable at Mrs Murphy's?'

'Oh aye,' Brendan said.

'Did you talk to Mr Castle?'

'He came to the Ivy Tree. I was there last night too. Miss Meikle sang.'

'She must be a nice singer,' Elizabeth said. 'I like her. She talks to me about Alec and she treats Ruth so naturally. She would make a good mother. Brendan, I'm sorry, I should never have treated you like that. The trouble is . . .'

She couldn't tell him what the trouble was, and Brendan didn't give her the chance to have two goes at it. He got hold of her and kissed her, and it was even better than it had been the first time. Stupidly, she knew, being so close to Brendan was like when she had been a little girl and would take her shoes and socks off and plunge her toes into the icy water of the stream below the village. She was not supposed to do such things, her mother had told her.

'I won't drink any more,' Brendan said.

'Don't make promises to me,' Elizabeth said, putting her arms around his neck. 'I'll take you as you are.'

Thirty-Four

Josh had forgotten how far it was to Bristol. Had it felt so far last time? Last time he had known he was coming back. This time he had no such promise. It took all the willpower he had to leave his family. His mother and father went to the station with him. They must be glad to get rid of him, he thought, considering who they were and the gossip. Why was life so complicated?

He was only glad when the train drew in and it was time to say goodbye. They did not embrace him but he could see them waving until the train left the station and then he had the day to get through remembering how it had been when he and Patience came north together, that awful day when they had not spoken after she had told him she had burned Emma's letters.

It was late when he arrived in Bristol, and he was not very surprised when none of the Matthews family was there to meet him. They had sent the carriage for him. It drew up in front of their tall neat Georgian house and he remembered clearly that Patience had run away from him. No doubt they thought she had good cause. He had never felt less welcome.

As he went in, Mrs Matthews appeared in the hall.

'Joshua. How lovely to see you,' was her greeting, but her eyes were cool. 'I'm afraid my husband had business today. Do sit down and I'll have some tea brought in.'

Josh wanted to ask after Patience, to say anything which might be considered even remotely intelligent, but he couldn't. He drank his tea, Mrs Matthews made polite conversation and after that he was shown to his room. It was not the same room as his wife's, it was quite clearly his, with no door leading to

196

another, as they had had on their wedding night, for all the good that was.

Dinner was to be at eight. Josh came downstairs just a little before that.

'Mr Matthews would like to see you in the library, sir,' the butler said.

Josh went in. Diarmud got up.

'Good evening,' he said. 'How is your family?'

'Very well, thank you.'

'Do take a seat. We all understand the position. You treated my daughter so badly that she ran away from you. You are only here now because of my influence and her persuasion. A minister who cannot look after or be kind to his wife is not an asset to the church.'

He paused. Josh said nothing. Diarmud waited and it occurred to Josh for the first time that he might get up and say he didn't care any more, that he didn't want to be a minister any longer, that he was tired of it all, so he had no idea who the person was who went on sitting there, as though any of it mattered. And then he thought back to Alec and Alec's old granny, and Brendan and Elizabeth. He got to his feet.

'My sole purpose in coming here was to try to win Patience back, and if she lets me, I will treat her well. Will you at least let me try?'

'I wouldn't have had you back here otherwise. My only child's happiness is the most important thing in my life. This is your last chance,' Diarmud said.

Patience came in to dinner just a trifle later than everyone else, as though she had planned it that way. She was pale and thin and wore an expensive dress and pearls and she looked like somebody else's wife, some rich man. He could not believe she was anything to do with him. She was also even more beautiful than he remembered her, and he wanted to tell her how much she mattered to him, how he had longed to be with her, but he couldn't, he had to go on eating and drinking.

After the meal, her parents very tactfully left them alone

in the drawing-room with the tea tray. Josh looked around at the splendour and admitted to himself that he had the feeling that if he did get her back he would be subjected to a very long time of Mr and Mrs Matthews and their indulgent lifestyle.

'How are Elizabeth and the baby?' Patience said.

Josh had not realized that she cared so much about the people she had left, or was it just something safe to talk about?

'I think Elizabeth and Brendan might get married.'

It was not just something to discuss. She gave a little cry of joy and said, 'Tell me all about it,' patting the sofa as she did so. He sat down and told her about them and about all the other people she knew, and how Elizabeth's mother had interfered and how Wes was enjoying working at the foundry, and how much better his father was.

'And Emma Meikle?'

'Emma's fine.'

There was an awkward little silence after that.

'Patience . . .' he started, but she interrupted him.

'I'm not going back there,' she said, and she looked him straight in the eyes. It's not the right place for me, and even though I'm your wife, I won't do it. I know you never cared for me as you cared for Emma, and I miss everybody. I miss your family and Elizabeth and the baby, but it isn't for me, not at that level of poverty. I can't do it, and if you insist on going back, you will have to go without me. I wish things had been different, but I have the feeling that if I had acted honourably in the first place, you would have gone back there and we would never have been married.'

'You've obviously given it a great deal of thought,' Josh said.

She got up.

'I haven't thought about anything else. I have missed you desperately, but I haven't been brought up to that kind of life. It might have been better had you not come here at all, you could have married Emma, she would have known nothing else and you would have been happy.'

'I couldn't have married her. I knew from the beginning

that it wouldn't happen, but I was so much in love with her. I thought there must be a way out. My parents were desperate to get me away from her.'

'And did they really succeed?'

'I want to be with you,' he managed.

She said nothing.

'Please . . .'

There was silence after that, and then she said, 'This may be possible, but there are conditions attached.'

'I thought there might be.'

'The first is that we live here with my parents in the way that they live, without you looking down your nose at the style of it. The second is –' she hesitated here and went pink – 'that we have a room each and that you don't come into my room until you're invited, and the third is that you accept with grace any appointment that you are offered. The only other thing is . . . that if you are ever unfaithful to me, either with Emma Meikle or with anyone else, it will be the finish.'

'Is that all?' Josh said, trying to keep the sarcasm out of his voice.

'Yes, that's everything. Do think about it.' And she left him there without even pouring out the tea.

Josh was too angry to consider it. He wanted to throw something or hit somebody. He didn't dare stay downstairs for fear he should meet her mother or father and say the wrong thing, so he went to bed. He wanted to tell her that he would not dream of being unfaithful to anybody, and then was assaulted by the knowledge that he had been unfaithful to his promise to Emma to come back and marry her, so he obviously couldn't rely on himself.

The following morning Diarmud asked him once more into the study and said, 'Patience told me that she had asked you to agree to certain terms. I take it you will?'

'Whatever she wishes,' Josh said softly.

Diarmud said no more, but took him to see the head of the conference in the area, and Josh learned that he was to have his first appointment, and as soon as was decently possible he would become superintendent of the local circuit.

'It's a very great privilege at your age,' he was told, 'but we realized when you had gone that we ought not to have let you go. It was neither your father's wish nor the best thing for the church – nor for you.'

By the time they got home, it was early evening and Patience had gone upstairs to dress. He went up and knocked on the door and when her maid answered, he said, 'May I come in?'

'Certainly,' Patience said.

He waited for her to dismiss the girl, and when she didn't he said, 'Did you hear about my new appointment?'

'My father told me. It's very nice for you.'

Josh looked at the girl who was brushing Patience's hair.

'Eve, would you mind leaving us for a few minutes? I'd like to talk to Mrs Castle alone.'

Patience waited until the girl had gone, and then she looked at him.

'Any other man would have just told her to go. You even remembered her name.'

'I always remember everybody's name.'

'I had noticed. It's very unfair to them, it makes them think you care when in fact you don't. It's just you displaying how brilliant you are. You don't need to recruit her, she's already a Methodist.'

'You always think I'm motivated that way.'

'You always are. You married me because you thought it would be a good thing for the church, instead of the girl you really wanted.'

'No, I didn't. I married you because I couldn't help it, because for the first time in my life something was more important to me than my calling.'

Patience stared.

'That's not true.'

'Yes, it is, I just wouldn't admit it to myself. I lost control. I couldn't not have married you.'

'But, having done it, you turned our marriage into a night-mare,' Patience protested. 'I know I behaved badly about the letters, but if you think I'm going to put up with the same kind of marriage, you're wrong, because I'm not. I don't want you under any illusions. My father's influence got you that position. You can't go to a poor community and exert your magic there, for your own self-satisfaction. You must do the work that only you can do.'

'That's what my father said.'

'He's a better man than you.'

'I know it.'

'Very well then,' Patience said, and she rang the bell to bring Eve back, and Josh had no choice but to go to his own room and change for dinner. Here Mr Matthews had already been busy, there were new clothes and a valet to help him. To dismiss him would possibly cost the man his job, so Josh accepted the help and then went down to dinner.

After they had eaten, her mother went off to see to someone who had called, and her father went to his study, and Patience said to him, in the privacy of the drawing room, 'You didn't speak a single word over the meal.'

'You mean you want conversation as well? Maybe you should tell me what you would like me to say. I wouldn't wish to be disagreeable.' And she leaned over and smacked his face.

It had been years and years since Josh had lost his temper. He thought he didn't have the kind of temper which got lost but he was wrong. He got hold of her and shook her.

'You nasty little bitch!'

'Don't you call me names.'

'What are you going to do, tell your father about it? Well?'

She pulled free and sat there, almost in tears, the curls at either side of her face falling forward to hide her emotion, the rest of her hunched and resentful. Josh took a deep breath. He couldn't believe he had behaved like this.

'You don't have to do this to me,' he said. 'I love you. Give me another chance, please.'

'You love me?'

'Yes, I do. I can't stand any more of this. Just one chance?'

She shook back the curls.

'Can I kiss you?' Josh said.

'Yes.'

He did but very carefully, very slowly, and after that she drew away and said that she was going to bed. She went. Josh walked up the stairs after her and went into his room.

He didn't go to bed. He did what he always did when things were particularly difficult, he sat down at the desk and wrote and tried not to admire the furnishings, the big bed which had already been turned down, the way he had only to ring for whatever he wanted, the street sounds outside, and he longed for the little vestry in the chapel at home and the reassurance of the people he was used to.

There was a soft knocking on the door. He assumed it was the valet come to see if he needed help, and he was trying to think how to refuse without seeming dismissive when the door opened and Patience came in. She was wearing something soft and blue. She hesitated by the door for a second and then banged it shut and came over and threw herself at him.

'I didn't mean any of it,' she said, rather muffled against his shoulder. 'I love you to distraction. There now, I've said it.'

Josh held her close, told her over and over again how much he loved her, and, after that, the loss of the ministry he had so much wanted for his own didn't seem quite so important. He must accept that he would never go back, at least not in the same way. He had lost forever the place in his family, the chapel and the people. He had the feeling that nothing would ever matter as much again.

Emma was sitting in the bar when she heard the noise in the darkness behind her.

'We're closed,' she said, without getting up.

'I should hope so. You can't go crying like that in front of the customers,' said Daniel Swinburne as he appeared from the shadows by the door. 'Has he gone? Is that the reason for the tears?'

'Daniel,' she said, smiling at him.

He came over, sat down at the table opposite to her.

'Would you like whisky?' she asked him.

'Don't get up.' He got up himself and went over to the bar,

where he found glasses and poured, and brought the glasses back and put one in front of her. She sipped it.

'Is it for good this time?' Daniel said.

'I think so, yes.'

She sat back in her chair. Emma made herself not cry any more. The whisky helped. They sat there in the quiet of the night and she thought how much she had missed him.

'Emma . . .' he said, and then stopped and looked at her.

'What?' she prompted him.

'I don't know how to say it or whether it's a good idea.'

'You don't know until you try,' Emma said.

'Yes. Well. I wondered if you might come to tea at my house on Sunday?'

'It sounds very nice,' Emma said. 'Yes, I will.'

Daniel hesitated and then he looked at her and said, 'My mother loved your father.'

And that was when Emma understood.

'And she used to sing the song for him?' she guessed.

'We were all going to run away.'

'What happened?'

'He met your mother and changed his mind.'

'I won't change my mind,' she said.

Daniel smiled. It was a good smile, it hit his eyes.

'Oh good,' he said.

Emma saw him to the door but as he opened it she said, 'Daniel . . .' and he stopped.

'What?'

'Will you come back tomorrow night?'

'If you want me to.'

'I do.' And she kissed him again very briefly but sweetly on the lips.

'Very well then, I will. See you tomorrow.'

When he had gone, she locked up and she heard footsteps behind her and Lucy stood just inside the door which led from the hall into the bar. Emma wasn't quite sure how long she had been within earshot.

'I suppose I'll have to run the place without you. I shall

203

expect to be chief bridesmaid,' Lucy said, and hugged her.

'Don't get your hopes up,' Emma said as she left the room.

'Oh, but I do. I do get my hopes up. I think perhaps we won't be old maids after all.' And she took the lamp and looked around the empty bar and then she closed the door and went to bed.